W

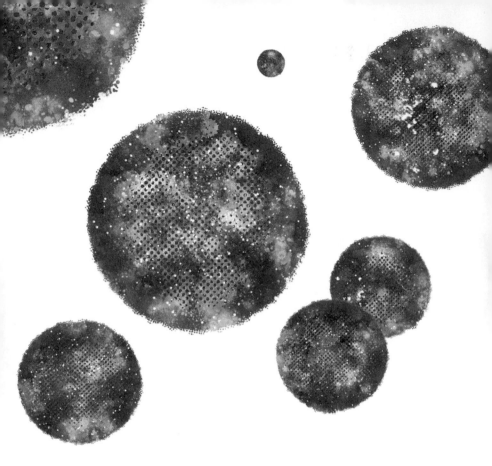

UNIVERSES 0/I, I/I, 2/I, I/2, 2/2, I/3, I/4 . . . I44/I . . . I45/I . . .

SOMETIMES PLANS DON'T WORK OUT.

Oftentimes inventions fail.

Who can know how things work out?

There is a theory that every possibility works out.

That there are multiple universes.

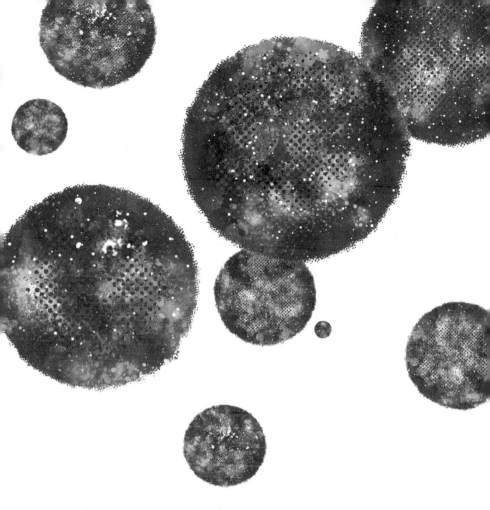

An infinite number of universes.

One for every combination of possibilities.

For the universe where you didn't make the bus this morning, you missed the class on stars, you weren't inspired to become a scientist, and the world didn't get the invention that you would go on to make, which would change everything . . .

ANK
TEIN

and the SPACE-TIME ZIPPER

JON SCIESZKA
ILLUSTRATED BY BRIAN BIGGS

AMULET BOOKS
NEW YORK

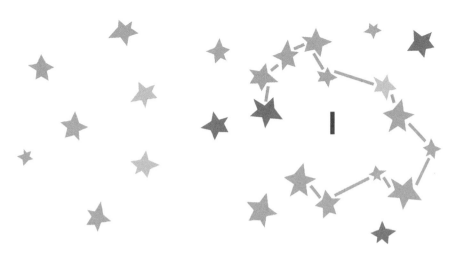

THE SUN SETS SLOWLY IN THE WESTERN SKY OF MIDVILLE.

Watson zips down East Oak Street as fast as he can pedal.

From the other side of town, Janegoodall races along West Oak Street.

They both hit the corner of Oak and Pine at almost exactly the same moment, skid, slide, turn, and stop.

Watson holds up his phone. "You got the weird text from Frank, too?"

Janegoodall nods. "What do you think it means?"

Watson shakes his head. "I have no idea what's going on . . . but it sounds like Frank's in trouble."

Janegoodall reads from her phone. "Need help. Come to junkyard. Follow the arrow sign. At sunset. Bring banana."

Watson holds up a slightly smushed banana.

Janegoodall shakes her head. "I have no idea."

Watson looks at the setting sun. "Let's roll!"

Watson and Janegoodall race their bikes to Grampa Al Einstein's house/Fix It! repair shop and Frank Einstein's laboratory.

They skid to a stop, drop their bikes, race around the back of Grampa Al's.

They scan the piles of junk.

"There," says Watson.

Janegoodall and Watson follow the old lightbulb-studded arrow sign.

But it points to nothing except a pile of broken toasters.

The red-orange rays of the setting sun light the top of the giant maple tree in the alley.

Watson jams the banana in his back pocket. "Frank needs help with . . . toasters?"

Janegoodall looks around. "Maybe this is the wrong sign."
She kicks at a pile of junk. She sees metal.

Janegoodall and Watson clear away the toasters. But the
metal turns out to be nothing but a storm drain.

A crow caws in the distance.

Venus, the evening star, glows silver in the gathering
dusk.

"Are we too late?"

"Maybe we missed sunset."

Janegoodall and Watson look up.

And that's when they hear a metallic clink. A knocking
on the storm sewer cover.

Watson and Janegoodall kneel down, use two rusted
metal rods to pry up the metal disk.

"Frank . . . ?"

SPACE.

Outer space.

Hundreds . . . no, thousands . . . no, millions of points of light dot the moonless inky blue-black night sky.

A kid wearing size-five brown wing-tip shoes swings a giant telescope in a slow arc. He scans the points of starlight.

"Wow!"

Standing next to the kid, a chimpanzee in a lab coat, pleasantly surprised for once, agrees.

The sparkly expanse of the Milky Way, splashed across the sky, is . . . wow.

"Look at all of those stars. All of those suns. So many planets."

Mr. Chimp nods.

"If we could find a way to travel out there . . . just think . . . we could . . ."

Mr. Chimp nods again, his mind expanding with thoughts of the sheer immensity of the universe. The sheer immensity of *possibilities*. He is glad he came back. Glad T. Edison might be of some help in his Big Plan.

". . . make so . . . much . . . money!"

Mr. Chimp covers his face with his hands.

If it weren't so dark in the rooftop observatory of Chimp-Edison Laboratories, you could see him shaking his head. Now less glad.

T. Edison shuts down his telescope. He closes up the observatory. He flicks on the lights.

"But other planets, other solar systems, are so far away."

T. Edison paces back and forth. He looks over his planet charts.

"It takes too many years to get anywhere."

Mr. Chimp slides his hands down his face. This is the first smart thing he has heard T. Edison say tonight.

Mr. Chimp signs:

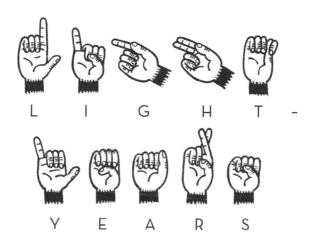

L I G H T -

Y E A R S

"Exactly!" says T. Edison. "The distance that light can travel, speeding nearly 300,000 kilometers per second." T. Edison starts pacing again. "I'll bet you didn't know that!"

Mr. Chimp sits down and writes out the mathematical formula for the distance of one light-year.

Mr. Chimp holds up his calculation.

This annoys T. Edison.

SPEED of LIGHT ×
60 SEC × 60 MIN
×24 HOURS
× 365 DAYS =
———————
ABOUT
6 TRILLION MILES

"Well, maybe you did know. But here is my genius idea—what if I invent a way to travel *faster* than light? Then we could get to any planet. In seconds. Like taking a train. A very fast train."

Mr. Chimp looks up from his calculations. He doesn't even know where to start.

He could remind T. Edison that nothing can outrace light.

He could explain to T. Edison that when a car traveling at the speed of light turns on its lights . . . the light still travels at the speed of light.

He could explain to T. Edison the vast scale of the universe.

That if Earth were the size of a tennis ball, the sun would be seven football fields away. The next closest star would be 130,000 miles away. The next galaxy unimaginably far away.

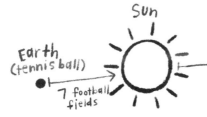

But Mr. Chimp is tired of explaining things to T. Edison.

Plus—this time, he's got a plan of his own.

Mr. Chimp gathers up his papers, looks at T. Edison, and lies:

Mr. Chimp waves good-night.

And heads off to his own room.

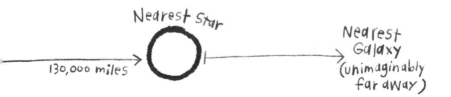

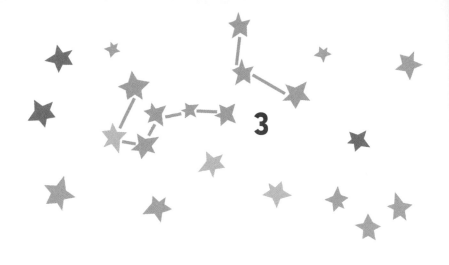

3

THE MIDVILLE STORM DRAIN COVER MOVES.

Watson and Janegoodall grab an edge, heave, and slide the heavy metal disc sideways.

Watson peers down into the shadowed tunnel.

In the fading sunlight, he sees a crazy mess of hair, a dirty lab coat, and two hands reaching up.

Watson and Janegoodall grab Frank's hands and pull.

"Frank!"

It is.

Frank Einstein.

Watson and Janegoodall pull Frank up out of the drain. He collapses in a heap next to Grampa Al's motorcycle and the pile of old toasters.

Frank sits up. "Amazing!" He weaves back and forth.

Frank looks up to the stars. His eyes close. He slumps over.

Watson and Janegoodall load Frank into a red wagon and take him inside to his lab. They lay him on the old couch in the corner. Watson wipes the dirt off his face. Janegoodall gets a cup of water.

Frank's eyes slowly open.

"Watson. Janegoodall. Thank goodness you made it."

"Of course we did," says Janegoodall. "What happened? Why were you down there?"

Frank lies back on the couch.

"Oh! And here's your banana," says Watson. He pulls the slightly mashed fruit out of his pocket.

Frank takes the banana. Peels it. And scarfs it down.

"What's the banana got to do with anything?" Watson asks.

"Is it because it contains vitamin C, potassium, and magnesium?" guesses Janegoodall.

Frank finishes the banana. "No, I was just hungry for a banana."

Watson shakes his head and laughs.

"Much better," says Frank. "This is so amazing. You are not going to *believe* where Grampa Al and I have been."

"Grampa Al?" asks Janegoodall.

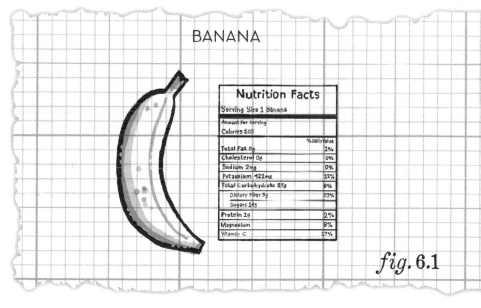

BANANA

Nutrition Facts
Serving Size 1 Banana

Amount Per Serving
Calories 105

	% Daily Value
Total Fat 0g	1%
Cholesterol 0g	0%
Sodium 2mg	0%
Potassium 422mg	12%
Total Carbohydrate 27g	9%
Dietary Fiber 3g	12%
Sugars 14g	
Protein 1g	2%
Magnesium	8%
Vitamin C	17%

fig. 6.1

"Is he in the other room getting his telescope?"

"Ummmmm, no."

"Then where is he? You were the only one in there."

Frank runs his hands through his electrified hair.

"Ohhhhh nooooooo. I lost Grampa Al."

"You *lost* him? In the sewer?"

"No," says Frank. "Worse. He accidentally fell into my space-time rip. Before my invention was ready."

"What?!" Watson exclaims.

"So where is he?" asks Janegoodall.

Frank looks up. "Come to the roof. I'll show you."

4

FRANK SWINGS THE BIG TELESCOPE ON THE ROOF OF GRAMPA AL'S to point north in the night sky. "Right near the constellation Cassiopeia. That big W shape . . ."

He adjusts the viewfinder, zeroing in on a pinpoint of light.

Watson and Janegoodall look at each other. They wonder if Frank Einstein has lost his mind.

"There!" says Frank. "Look."

Watson looks. "What am I looking at?"

"Alpha Andromedae. Brightest star in the Andromeda constellation. Ninety-seven light-years away."

"And why are we looking there?"

"Grampa Al. He's somewhere near there."

Now Watson and Janegoodall are sure Frank has lost his mind.

"Really. Ninety-seven light-years away?"

"Yes, yes." Frank brushes them off.

"But . . . how did you get ninety-seven light-years away? And back again? Even if you were traveling at the speed of light, it would have taken you . . ."

"About one hundred ninety-four years," figures Janegoodall.

"So much work to do . . ." mutters Frank. He scratches his head. He sketches on a blank sheet of graph paper. "Albert Einstein's happiest thought—gravity is simply the warping of space-time. Small object causes small distortion of space-time. Massive object causes massive distortion. Simple!"

"Frank!" Janegoodall snaps him out of it. "What are you talking about? You are not making any sense."

Frank looks down at the lines he has scribbled on the paper.

"Einstein's general theory of relativity. Space, time, gravity . . . all connected. All part of the same thing. That's how to travel farther and faster than the speed of light. But something went wrong . . ."

"What?"

Frank doesn't answer. He keeps talking to himself out loud. "All connected. Maybe a different way. Maybe. Like this."

Frank draws a crazy mess of circles and lines that look mostly like an octopus putting on socks.

"See? All connected. Just have to maybe re-power the crossover circuits to use space-time bend. Get Grampa Al back!"

Jane and Watson study the crazy diagram.

They look at Frank all wild-eyed and wobbly on his feet.

"Ummmmm, right," says Jane. "But maybe a bit of sleep first."

Frank looks up at the stars. He pats his pockets, looking for something. "Oh no. No time to waste. Time is space. Space is time. Connect time and space."

Frank spins around in a slow circle, still patting his pockets. "Must. Save. Grampa Al. Now."

Watson takes Frank by the arm and gently steers him away from the edge of the rooftop.

Frank blinks, closes one eye.

"Right . . . now . . ."

Frank falls forward, asleep on his feet, right into Watson's arms.

Watson looks at Janegoodall. "Did any of that make any sense?"

Janegoodall looks down at Frank's crazy diagram, and up at the stars. "No . . . and yes . . ."

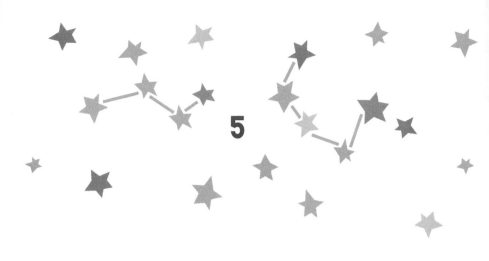

5

CAMEROON, AFRICA, 1956

Deep in the jungle, a baby chimpanzee is born.
The world turns. The sun rises and sets.
Men! With nets.

They come and scoop up baby into a cage, a metal flying machine, across an expanse of water bigger than anything

a chimp could imagine.

But this chimp is curious. This chimp looks around.

Space camp. Training. Forty chimps.

Simple humans. They wonder if a chimp can press a lever. For a small banana pellet and sip of water. Wrong answer, shock on the feet.

G-forces. Funny suit. Spinning upside down. Locked in a cradle.

Now only eighteen chimps.

Only female is Minnie.

More tests.

Now only six.

Minnie still here.

Something big is up. Only two chosen for this mission. Ham and Minnie.

Now just one.

Number 65.

Ham.

Night.

Cradle.

Capsule on top of giant rocket.

Something is wrong. Six-hour delay.

Dawn. Go.

Blastoff roar. G-forces, just like in training, but even more.

Lights . . . flip lever.

Now 155 miles above Earth.

Capsule separates from rocket.

Lights . . . flip lever.

Weightless for five minutes.

Lights . . . flip lever.

Directional rockets position capsule for reentry.

Screaming/heat/bang.

Lights . . . flip lever.

At 18 minutes after launch, capsule splashes into ocean.

But it has shot too far off course. The broken heat shield has poked a hole in the capsule. Water splashing inside, filling up capsule.

Helicopter comes in the nick of time.

On the ship. Capsule opened. Cradle opened.

Apple and half an orange.

Ham the Astrochimp. Space Hero. The first primate in space. Proving that man should be able to survive going into space.

MAY 1961

Four months after Ham's voyage, astronaut Alan Shepard rides the same kind of rocket, in the same kind of Mercury capsule, to become the first American in space.

Back at ChimpEdison Labs, the grandson of Ham and Minnie puts his papers back in the chest. He takes out a yellow safety helmet and puts it on his head. He picks up an old control lever device and tucks it under his arm.

Mr. Chimp looks up into the night sky and signs to his long-gone hero chimp grandpa.

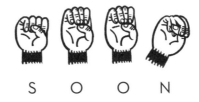

S   O   O   N

6

AT 8:34 AM EASTERN STANDARD TIME, AN ALARM CLOCK GOES OFF.
And because this is inventor Frank Einstein's alarm clock **(A)**, of course it doesn't go off by simply ringing.

It goes off by way of a hammer **(B)** on top of an old alarm clock smacking a nail **(C)** . . . that knocks a peg **(D)** . . . that frees a ten-speed bicycle gear **(E)** . . . that drops a little barbell on the end of a chain **(F)** . . . that turns another gear **(G)** . . . and a wheel **(H)** . . . and another and another and another in a maze of interlocking gears **(I)** and wheels **(J)** covering the entire wall until the last wheel **(K)** turns a worm gear . . . that spins a metal rod **(L)** . . . that opens the vertical floor-to-ceiling blinds . . . filling the room with bright morning sun.

Frank sits up and scratches his head with both hands.

Frank slowly gets the distinct feeling that all of this has happened before.

Then Frank smells pancakes.

Grampa Al! He must have made it back!

Frank throws on jeans, a T-shirt, and lab coat. He slides on shoes, no socks, and hustles down to the kitchen behind the Fix It! repair shop.

Frank zips past the walls covered with Grampa Al's charts and diagrams of *The Phases of the Moon*, and *The*

Constellations. He takes a left down the hall of *Tectonic Plates* and *The Geological Timescale.* He takes a right past *The Human Skeletal System* and *The Circulatory System.*

He hops onto the *Double Helix DNA* slide, spirals down two floors, and pops through the *Plant-Cell/Animal-Cell* swinging doors right into the kitchen.

"Good morning, Einstein," says the cook, scooping pancakes out of a frying pan.

Frank answers, "Good morning . . . ohhh . . . Watson?"

Because it's not Grandpa Al in the kitchen. It's Watson. And Janegoodall.

Watson serves Frank, Janegoodall, and himself each a steaming stack of pancakes. He turns on the carbon-atom light fixture above the table. It glows with a funny mix of six blue proton and six red neutron lights in the center nucleus, surrounded by six occasionally blinking white electron lights.

Frank sits down and rubs his head with both hands.

He is sure all of this has happened before.

"How? . . . Wha? . . ."

"Eat first," says Janegoodall. "Then you can explain everything. And then we can get to work."

Frank nods. He eats a delicious mouthful of warm pancake, melted butter, and maple syrup. This is a great idea. Frank had no idea he was this hungry.

The carbon-atom light glows over the kitchen table.

The three friends eat in happy silence.

• • •

Frank finishes the last of his pancakes. He looks up. And sees the framed photo of Grampa Al winning the Midville Science Prize for his super electromagnet.

Frank can't wait any longer.

"So, Grampa Al didn't turn up last night?"

Watson shakes his head.

"Ohhh man," says Frank. "It's all my fault. The transport invention wasn't ready. I shouldn't have set it up there. How would Grampa Al know?"

Frank taps his fork on his plate, thinking out loud. "Transistor . . . resistor . . . reverse the poles . . . maybe crosswire the fantods . . . He might have gotten stranded on that white dwarf. What if he's getting twisted in another? We have to go *now*!"

"Wait!" says Janegoodall. "You're talking gibberish again. And you're not going to do Grampa Al any good going off half-cocked like this. Now sit down. Tell us what happened."

"Yeah," says Watson. "We can fix this."

Frank runs his fingers through his hair. He takes a deep breath. "Right. I was working on a transport invention, to travel faster than the speed of light and explore deeper in space."

Watson nods and wisecracks, "Sure. Like everyone does."

Frank doesn't notice.

"I had the Space-Time Transporter set up out back in Grampa Al's junkyard. And I forgot to tell him it was there. I powered the Space-Time Transporter up to test it. And I had to go back to my lab for a wrench. I left for just a second. And—"

Frank looks down at his empty plate.

Watson looks horrified. "Oh no! You killed Grampa Al?!"

"No no no. He just tried the Space-Time Transporter before it was ready. Or maybe it used too much power. Because I followed him. We both made it to Alpha Andromedae. But only I made it back."

"Whew," says Watson. "But also—that's nuts!"

Janegoodall taps her fork on her plate, thinking. "Well, if you weren't Frank Einstein, I would say this was completely crazy. But the answer to this is pretty clear. We have to get your invention up and running again to save Grampa Al."

Frank smiles. He loves that he can always count on Janegoodall. "Exactly," says Frank. "But we are going to need more brainpower."

"Of course," says Janegoodall. "And you have the absolute best helpers. Klink and Klank."

Frank looks surprised. "Klink! And Klank!"

"Yeah, you remember them," says Watson sarcastically. "Your robot pals. One small, one big. One smart, one—"

"Oh no!" Frank jumps to his feet. "I completely forgot about Klink and Klank! They are *not* going to be happy."

Frank runs to his lab.

He gets that same sharp memory/feeling of having done all of this before.

He remembers the time he first walked into his lab and heard the electronic voice of a robot that was alive.

This time, he knows they are alive . . . but he hopes he is not too late.

7

FRANK FUMBLES WITH A KEY IN THE BATHROOM DOORKNOB.

"What in the world are you doing?" asks Janegoodall.

"It's the only door that has a lock," answers Frank. "I had to keep them safe in here."

"Hmmmmmmum," says Janegoodall, rolling her eyes and shaking her head.

"There!" Frank turns the key and swings open the door.

The big robot sitting on the toilet looks up from his comic book.

"Frank! Janegoodall! Watson! It is so good to see you."

Klank holds up the book he was reading.

"Have you read this very amazing book? There is a big cat. He does not like to work. But he does love to eat. Mostly lasagna."

The small robot, squeezed in the corner, crosses his arms in front of his Shop-Vac chest. And does not say anything.

"I am so sorry I had to lock you guys in here," says Frank. "And then forgot about you last night."

Klink's single webcam eye stares at Frank.

"I didn't want to take the chance of your electronics getting destroyed in space-time travel," continues Frank. "But Grampa Al got sidetracked on the return. So we have to fix the transport invention to find him and bring him back. Come on in the lab. And let's get started."

Klank tucks his comic book under one flex-tube arm and squeezes his big trash-can body out of the teeny bathroom.

"Gosh, this sounds exciting."

"Great!" says Frank. "Come on, Klink. You can give Watson and Janegoodall the background they need on solar systems, stars and galaxies, and gravitational forces. Klank and I will start rebuilding the portal."

Everyone heads for Frank's laboratory.

Everyone except Klink.

Klink does not move.

Klink says, "No."

"Huh?" says Watson.

"No," repeats Klink. "This does not help me in any way. In fact, it may be dangerous to me. I will stay right here."

"But we need you," says Watson.

Klink keeps his arms folded. "Everyone did just fine without me for the last . . . oh, twenty-three point five hours."

Janegoodall puts a hand on top of Klink's glass-dome head. "But Klink, you are the smartest robot. Of course we need you. Please come and help us."

Klink hums. He swivels his webcam eye back and forth.

"No. And, Klank, you might want to think about what always happens to you when you try to help."

Klank stops, looks back.

"Like what?"

Klink flashes. "Like the first time we ran into T. Edison. And his Antimatter Squirt Gun blew you to bits."

"Oooh yeah. That was bad."

"Or the second time when you got chopped to bits by Edison's Hydroelectric Turbine.

"Ouch. I forgot about that."

"Or the third time when the BrainTurbo exploded your head."

Klank unconsciously touches his colander head.

"I am not even going to remind you what happened with the EvoBlaster Belt."

Klank remembers.

"Hey, yeah. This is not good for me."

"Fine!" says Frank. "Be that way, Klink. We don't need your help. We will fix the Space-Time Transporter without you."

Klank is not so sure. **"Can we?"**

"Yes," says Frank. He turns and stomps into the lab.

"But I do have one question."

"Yes?" asks Watson.

"What is lasagna?"

8

TEDISON LEANS OVER THE WORKTABLE IN THE CENTER OF TEST Room No. 3 of ChimpEdison Laboratories, adjusting the settings on two medium-size titanium boxes.

Mr. Chimp sits at one of the side tables, reading and double-checking his equations.

Igor, the laboratory cat, curls in the one padded chair, sleeping.

"Ohhhhhh yes!" says T. Edison.

He sets the dial on Box 1 to **OUTPUT**.

He sets the dial on Box 2 to **INPUT**.

He pushes the small door flaps on the front of both boxes to make sure they swing free. He slides the top view ports smoothly back and forth.

"Observe . . . and prepare to be amazed, Mr. Chimp," T. Edison brags. "I am about to change the universe. With my new T. Edison FasterThanTheSpeedOfLight Transport Device invention."

Mr. Chimp looks up from his book and signs sarcastically:

G R E A T

N A M E

T. Edison misses the sarcasm completely. "Why, thank you, Mr. Chimp. I thought it up all by myself."

Mr. Chimp shakes his head.

"With this new invention, I will be able to move objects across space in a way that is way faster than rockets. It works by moving across space-time. First objects. And then—people. We will be able to explore our galaxy, other galaxies, the whole universe . . . without waiting millions of years!"

Now Mr. Chimp is interested. He hadn't realized T. Edison was working on space-time travel, too. Mr. Chimp hops off his chair and takes a look.

"Watch . . . and learn."

T. Edison slides the titanium boxes apart.

He positions the door flaps so they face each other.

He flips the **ON** switch. *Hummmmmmm.*

Igor wakes to the sound, lifts his head.

T. Edison takes an apple and places it, through the door flap, inside Box 1.

He pushes the **SEND** button.

A subsonic hum—like a whale call, or an elephant cry you can't exactly hear but can feel in your bones—fills the room.

Igor sits up, alert now, ears back.

T. Edison turns **OFF** Box 1. He goes to Box 2. Reaches in. Pulls out . . . an apple stem.

"Ha! Eureka! Excelsior! Cowabunga!"

Mr. Chimp is surprised. T. Edison is actually onto something.

"Well, that worked pretty much perfectly. Now . . . for the *real* test!"

T. Edison walks over to the padded chair and picks up Igor.

Igor squirms and tries to hold on to the chair with his claws.

"Gooooood kitty. Niiiiiice kitty. Don't worry. What could happen?"

Mr. Chimp shakes his head.

"What do you mean, *no*?"

Mr. Chimp holds up his book.

"Yeah yeah yeah. I know. Einstein, relativity, space, time, and all that. But I can't be bothered to read every little thing."

T. Edison tries to push Igor into Box 1 through the Iris Aperture.

Igor spreads his legs and does everything he can to not fit in the box.

"Come on, kitty kitty," T. Edison sweet-talks Igor.

Igor is not buying any of it. He sinks his back claws into T. Edison's arm.

"*Yowwwwwch!*" T. Edison drops his fake-nice voice. "Get in there, you stupid cat. This is for science!"

T. Edison crams Igor in Box 1.

Yowling and sounds of smacking around come from inside the box.

T. Edison quickly flips the **ON** button, punches the **SEND** button.

HUMMMMMMMMMMMM elephant/whale hum.

Quiet.

Mr. Chimp looks at T. Edison.

"See, I told you it would work."

T. Edison turns off Box 1.

"I am going to be sooo famous. And sooooo rich."

T. Edison pats the top of Box 2. "Come on, my little Igor kitty. See, I told you there was nothing to worry about."

T. Edison reaches inside. He feels around. He grabs.

He pulls out one very small tuft of Igor fur.

Mr. Chimp raises one eyebrow.

Mr. Chimp decides it's time to fire up his own invention.

FRANK EINSTEIN LEANS OVER THE WORKTABLE OF HIS LABORATORY inside Grampa Al's garage. He fiddles with his Space-Time Transporter invention, muttering to himself.

Janegoodall and Watson sit on the other side.

Frank accidentally snaps off a connector rod. "Ach! This thing is a mess!"

Janegoodall reattaches the piece. "Frank?"

"What."

"Are you mad at Klink?"

Frank frowns. "No. Why should I be mad at Klink?"

"Ohh, maybe because he said he won't help you . . . ? And because you are worried about Grampa Al . . . ?"

"That is ridiculous. Who cares about Klink's help? We can fix this and find Grampa Al ourselves."

"I'm not so sure about that," says Watson.

The sound of robot laughs comes from the other room.

"We don't need that bossy pile of Klink parts. Grampa Al has all we need in his workshop. Come on. Let's go."

Frank Einstein stomps off to Grampa Al's workshop.

Janegoodall and Watson follow.

Klank's deep mechanical laugh echoes through the shop.

"HA HA HA HA . . ."

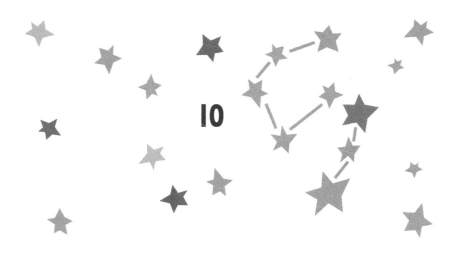

10

A H AH AH AH," BOOMS KLANK. "AH-CHOOO!" KLANK SITS DOWN. **"I think I am allergic to toast."**

Klink bonks Klank on the head. "Do not be ridiculous. Robots cannot be allergic. We are better than that."

"Okay," says Klank. **"AHHHHHH-CHOO!"**

Klink and Klank plug themselves into different outlets. They watch shark videos on the internet. They eat radio waves. They toast more bread.

"See? This is fun."

Klank flips the bread over. **"Yeah, I guess so."**

"No 'guess so' about it," says Klink. "This is so much more fun without humans telling us what to do.

We can look up anything. Do anything. Be anything."

Klank holds up his toast. **"But we do not even eat toast. I wish Watson was here. He loves toast."**

Klink's head bulb flashes red. "Forget the stupid toast! We are taking today off. And we are going to do whatever we want."

Klank jumps up. **"Oh good!"**

"That is more like it! You can do any fun robot thing you want. What do you want to do?"

Klank beams. **"I want to take this toast to Watson."**

Klink says, "No."

"And read my funny cat book to Janegoodall."

Klink says, "No."

"And give Frank Einstein a biiiiiiiig hug."

"Rrrrrrrrrrrrrrrrrrrr," Klink growls. "No. No. No."

Klank sits back down. He reads another page of his Garfield book.

Klink entertains himself solving math problems with one hand and building a scale model of the Voyager 1 space probe with the other.

"Klink?"

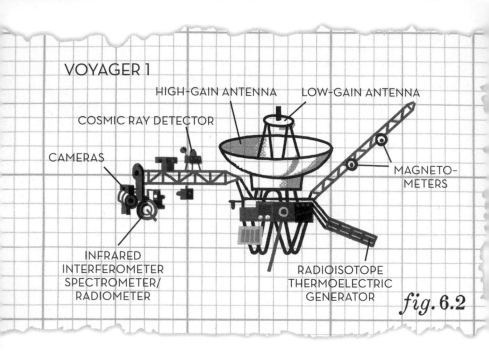

VOYAGER 1

HIGH-GAIN ANTENNA LOW-GAIN ANTENNA

COSMIC RAY DETECTOR

CAMERAS

MAGNETO-
METERS

INFRARED
INTERFEROMETER
SPECTROMETER/
RADIOMETER

RADIOISOTOPE
THERMOELECTRIC
GENERATOR

fig. 6.2

"What?"

"Do you know what is Garfield's favorite time?"

"No. Why would I know that?"

Klank waits. Klank smiles.

"Okay—what is Garfield's favorite time?"

"Time to sleep. HA. HA. HA."

Klink calculates.

"Why is that funny? Is it because time is part of space?"

"HA. HA. HA. No, I do not think so. I think he just loves to sleep. 'Time to sleep'—get it?"

Klink's brain circuits sizzle. He does not get it. "Grrrrrr."

BZZZZT! Klink's new circuit breaker switches his brain loop off . . . and saves his head from blowing up.

Klank blowtorches another piece of bread. **"Klink, are you mad at Frank?"**

Klink squints his one eye. "No. Why should I be mad at Frank?"

"Ohh, maybe because you do not think he is sorry enough for forgetting us in the bathroom . . . ?" says Klank.

"That is ridiculous. I just think we can do more fun things on our own."

Klank leafs through his Garfield book. **"I am not so sure about that."**

Klink and Klank hear Frank, Watson, and Janegood-all running through the garage, heading for Grampa Al's workshop.

"And it sounds like they are having fun."

Klink scowls.

"We are having more fun. Plug yourself back into those shark videos. Now!"

FRANK SHUFFLES THROUGH THE STACK OF BOOKS AND PAPERS ON Grampa Al's workbench.

"It must be here somewhere . . ."

Janegoodall picks up a small silver metal ball with four backswept antennas.

"Sputnik," says Watson.

"Gesundheit."

"No, that's the name of the thing you are holding—Sputnik. The first human-made object in space," says Watson. "Launched by the Russians in 1957. Orbited Earth for three months."

"Who knew you were such a space rocket nerd?" marvels Janegoodall. "What's that one?"

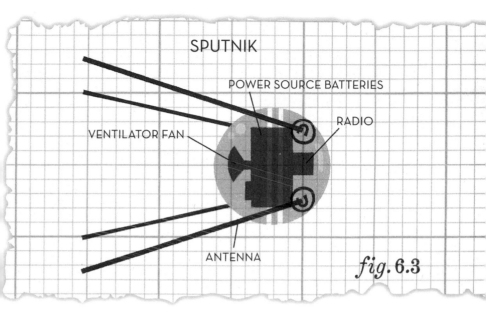

SPUTNIK

POWER SOURCE BATTERIES

RADIO

VENTILATOR FAN

ANTENNA

fig. **6.3**

"The Hubble Space Telescope," answers Watson. "Launched into orbit in 1990. Still operating. It takes the most amazing pictures because it's outside of Earth's atmosphere, so there's no distortion."

Frank leafs through Grampa Al's notebooks. "'Something . . . something about space-time fold . . .' is the last thing he said."

Ping . . . ping . . . ping . . . rings the model of the Mercury space capsule. Its bottom heat shield lights up red with each ring.

"I didn't touch it!" says Janegoodall. "Is it getting ready to blast off? Blow up?!"

Frank picks up the *pinging* space capsule.

"Nah. Grampa Al just rewired the phone. Again." Frank flips open the hatch door, holds the Mercury model up to his ear, and answers, "Al Einstein's Fix It! repair shop. Don't toss it. We'll fix it."

"Oh, hello sweetie. I was hoping we might catch you here," comes a voice out of the Mercury capsule top.

"Oh, hi, Mom."

"We tried your phone. But only got some very strange static."

Frank scratches his head. "Yeah, I think something funny happened to it in the space-time continuum . . ."

"In the what?"

Frank looks panicked. "Oooh, I mean . . . I think Watson accidentally broke it trying to be funny."

Watson frowns. Frank shrugs sorry.

"And we are uh . . . fixing it in Grampa's space . . . this time . . ."

"Well, that's nice. Your father and I just wanted to call and tell you we arrived safely in China. And that this is just one of the most amazing sites we have ever found for Travelalllovertheplace.com."

"The Great Wall?"

"No. The biggest radio telescope in the world! Five hundred meters wide. With a surface area as big as fifty football fields. And it's built into a natural bowl in the mountains out here."

Watson grabs the Mercury phone. "Are you kidding? That is twice as big as any other radio telescope!"

"Oh, hello, Watson," says Mom Einstein. "Yes, that's exactly right. The official name of the telescope is FAST. For Five-hundred-meter Aperture Spherical radio Telescope. But I like the Chinese nickname for it—Tianyan. The Eye of Heaven."

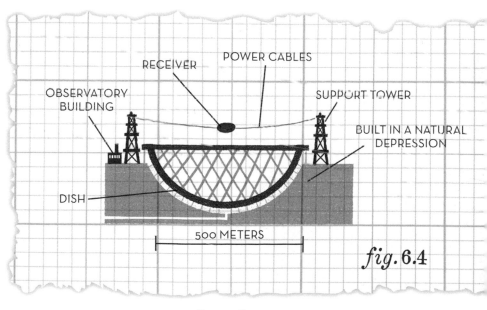

RECEIVER POWER CABLES
OBSERVATORY BUILDING
SUPPORT TOWER
BUILT IN A NATURAL DEPRESSION
DISH
500 METERS

*fig.*6.4

"Wow!"

A deeper voice comes out of the Mercury speaker.

"And *ni-hao* to you, too!" says Dad Einstein. "This baby is a beauty! And they have already detected radio signals from space as far away as one thousand light-years."

Frank's eyes light up.

"If there are any aliens out there in the universe, this thirty-ton dish is sure to hear their signal."

Frank grabs the Mercury capsule phone back from Watson.

"Hi, Dad. What was that you just said?"

"If there are any aliens—"

"No, the thing before that about a thousand light-years."

"Oh, yeah. That was one of the first signals the scientists here recorded. From one thousand light-years away."

Frank scratches his head again, like he always does when he gets an idea.

"Hey, is Grampa around? Mom and I wanted to ask him a couple of radio telescope questions."

Frank panics again. "Uhh yeah . . . I mean no . . . I mean he's not here. I mean right now . . . he's not here. He is . . . around . . . But ummm . . . not . . . right . . . here. Exactly now."

"Whaaaaat?" says Dad Einstein.

Janegoodall rolls her eyes and shakes her head. She takes the Mercury phone away from Frank.

"Hello, Mr. Einstein. This is Frank's friend Janegoodall."

"Oh hi, Janegoodall. Nice to hear your voice again. How is your baseball season and your monkey research going?"

"Very well," answers Janegoodall. "But at this very moment Frank and Watson and I are working on a very secret science project. Sorry we can't tell you any more over this unprotected phone line. We will have your father, Albert, ring you later, if that's OK."

"Oh, great," says Dad Einstein. "Well, good luck with your super-secret science project. *Zai jian!*"

"*Zai jian,*" says Janegoodall, and hangs up the Mercury phone.

Frank smiles. "Thanks for that save, Janegoodall. Now we *really* have to find Grampa Al, and soon." Frank taps his teeth. "And I think that giant Chinese radio telescope has given me an idea how we start . . ."

12

HIMPEDISON LABORATORIES.

Test Room X.

Mr. Chimp straps on the scuffed yellow safety helmet with a distinctive blue label.

He settles himself into his custom built—to exactly match his grandfather's—Space-Time pod.

He checks his levels. Adjusts his temp level.

The third lever lights up with a blue glow.

Mr. Chimp, just like his grandfather Ham more than fifty years ago, flicks the third lever down.

Something rumbles.

Something roars.

The clock on Mr. Chimp's desk picks up speed. Spins fast, faster, faster still.

The clock on Mr. Chimp's control fan ticks steady.

A rip, a tear.

Blackness.

The pod wobbles, jolts, groans. Something is wrong.

Mr. Chimp flicks levers madly . . . exactly according to plan and history.

Columns of light bend.

The rumble and roaring sounds squeal high, then low.

Then quiet.

Mr. Chimp releases the levers in his pod.

He pops off the top. And steps out.

He is back in Test Room X.

Mr. Chimp takes off his grandfather's helmet. He staggers a bit, catches himself, takes a banana out of his desk drawer, and devours it.

He checks his watch against his office clock.

His watch reads that he has been gone for nine minutes.

His office clock reads that he has been gone for nine hours.

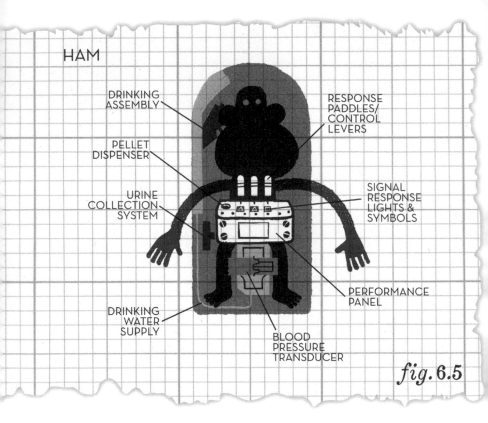

HAM

DRINKING ASSEMBLY

RESPONSE PADDLES/ CONTROL LEVERS

PELLET DISPENSER

URINE COLLECTION SYSTEM

SIGNAL RESPONSE LIGHTS & SYMBOLS

DRINKING WATER SUPPLY

PERFORMANCE PANEL

BLOOD PRESSURE TRANSDUCER

fig. **6.5**

Mr. Chimp smiles. It worked. Just like his Grampa Ham had secretly written. Almost. It just needs to be a little better.

The pod needs work. Needs some thoughtful improvement.

Mr. Chimp falls back on his chair.

Nothing has changed.

But everything has.

13

TEDISON PACES AROUND THE WORKTABLE IN TEST ROOM NO. 3. HE stops, crosses his arms, and stares at the two titanium boxes.

He thinks. He thinks.

He thinks some more.

"Aha!" he says out loud. Accidentally. To no one.

T. Edison unplugs the power pack of both T. Edison FasterThanTheSpeedOfLight Transport Devices.

He waits thirty seconds.

He plugs the power cords back into both T. Edison Faster-ThanTheSpeedOfLight Transport Devices.

The small windows in the corners of the boxes display faintly lit letters spelling:

REBOOT

T. Edison paces around the table.

The letters blink:

REBOOT

T. Edison sits down on the lab stool.

The letters blink:

REBOOT

T. Edison crosses his legs, taps his fingers on the table, pulls his ear.

The letters blink:

REBOOT
REBOOT
REBOOT
REBOOT
REBOOT
REBOOT
REBOOT
REBOOT

T. Edison holds his head in his hands.

The letters disappear and change to display the time:

12:48

"Finally!"

T. Edison jumps up, and powers **ON** both T. Edison Faster-ThanTheSpeedOfLight Transport Devices.

He takes an apple and places it, through the door flap, inside Box 1.

He turns the Box 2 dial to **INPUT**.

He presses Box 1's **SEND**.

The deep subsonic hum fills the lab.

Spiraling work icon.

It stops.

T. Edison reaches inside Box 2. And pulls out . . .

. . . a thin, shriveled, blackened sliver of apple skin.

"Ooooookayyyyy," says T. Edison. "Better . . ."

T. Edison ups the Gravity dial, loads a test tube in Box 1, presses **SEND**.

He pulls out of Box 2 . . . a small glass marble.

"Arrrrrrgh!"

Reset Box 1 to **SLOW ROAST**.

Load pencil.

SEND. *Hummmmmmm . . .*

Tiny eraser.

"Noooo!"

Reset to **PULSAR**.

Safety goggles.

SEND. *Hummmmmmmm . . .*

Strap.

"Grrrrrrrrrr!"

Water Bottle . . . *hummmmmmmm* . . . Water bottle cap.

Shoe . . . *hummmmmmmm* . . . shoelace.

Cheese sandwich . . . *hummmmmmmm* . . . crust.

T. Edison beats and pounds and smacks on the top of the T. Edison FasterThanTheSpeedOfLight Transport Device Box 1, shouting "No! No! No!"

The power light blinks **OFF**.

"Oh great," says T. Edison. "Now what, genius?"

T. Edison fumes.

T. Edison thinks . . . "Genius? Hmmm, I think I should pay a visit to some 'friends.'"

14 A

"So, to start from the beginning," says Frank Einstein, "our planet Earth is –"

"The third planet from our sun," says Janegoodall. "Earth is one of eight planets we currently count as our solar system:

"Mercury, Venus, Earth, Mars, Jupiter, Saturn, Uranus, and Neptune.

"They can be easily remembered in order with the sentence: My Very Excellent Mother Just Served Us Noodles."

Frank nods.

"Scientists think there may be a ninth planet, Planet X. But it has not yet been discovered.

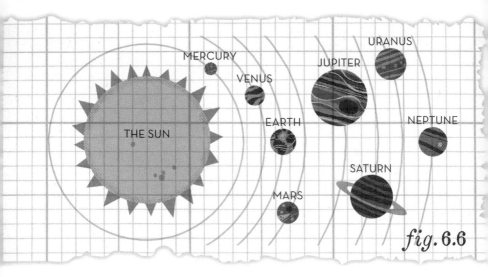

fig. 6.6

"Our solar system also contains 5 dwarf planets, over 140 moons, more than 3,000 comets, and at least 700,000 asteroids."

"Uhhhhhm . . . yes," says Frank, turning back to the posters on the Wall of Science. "And our sun—"

Janegoodall takes over again. "Is actually just a medium-size star. A ball of mostly hydrogen, and some helium gas. The nuclear reaction in the sun's core, of small hydrogen atoms fusing to make bigger helium atoms, produces all of the heat and light energy that the sun emits.

"With a surface temperature over 5,000 degrees Celsius, it's a good thing the sun is ninety-three million miles from Earth."

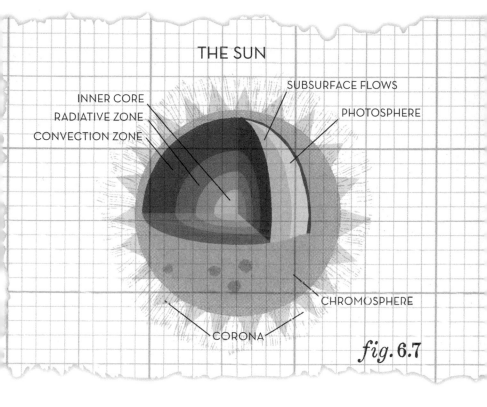

THE SUN

INNER CORE
RADIATIVE ZONE
CONVECTION ZONE

SUBSURFACE FLOWS
PHOTOSPHERE

CHROMOSPHERE

CORONA

fig. 6.7

"Right . . ." Frank begins.

Janegoodall continues, "*And* the electrical currents in the sun generate a crazy magnetic field we can't see. But most amazing is that the sun is such a massive body--over 99 percent of everything in the solar system is our sun—that its gravitational pull holds our whole solar system together."

Watson laughs. " 'Most amazing' is right."

Frank sits down, looking a bit stunned. "Uhhhh yeah. 'Amazing' is right. But how do you know all this?"

Janegoodall gives Frank a look. "You nutter. You do remember, don't you, that my mom works for NASA? And that I have been doing my school science reading."

"Yeah," adds Watson, still laughing at Frank. "You nutter."

14 B

"Soooo . . . traveling out beyond our solar system, the sun is . . ." Frank pauses, and looks to Janegoodall.

Janegoodall quickly continues, ". . . just one of at least 100 billion stars in the Milky Way galaxy.

"All of the stars orbit a gigantically massive black hole—about four million times as massive as our sun—in the center of the galaxy, in a spiral shape with four main arms.

"Our solar system is located in one of the four spiral arms of the galaxy." Janegoodall points to the spot on Grampa Al's Milky Way poster.

"And it takes about 230 million years for our solar system to orbit all the way around the center."

Frank sits down at the lab table.

"Whaaaaaa haaaa?" marvels Watson, shaking his head.

"Yes," says Janegoodall. "And the Milky Way is only one of more than ten trillion galaxies . . . that we can observe."

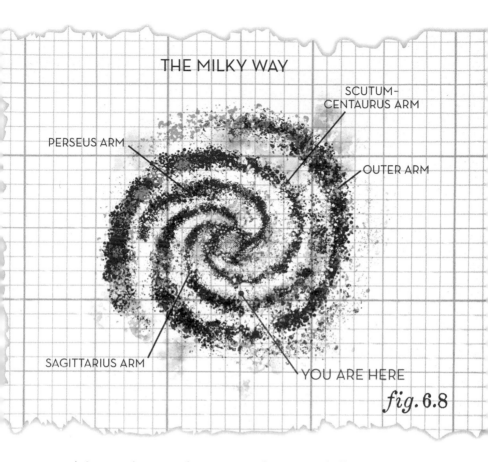

THE MILKY WAY

SCUTUM-
CENTAURUS ARM

PERSEUS ARM

OUTER ARM

SAGITTARIUS ARM

YOU ARE HERE

*fig.*6.8

Frank jumps in. "So there are at least 100 billion stars in each of maybe 100 trillion galaxies, making . . ."

Watson calculates, ". . . a whooooole lot of stars, solar systems, and planets."

"That we know of right now," adds Janegoodall. "The more we explore, the odds are we will discover more stars and solar systems and planets. Or maybe something even crazier. Who knows what is out there."

Watson whistles. "Something even *more* crazy than a trillion billion stars in the universe?"

Frank doesn't even pretend to start to explain.

He nods at Janegoodall, and she explains, "Like everything else in the universe, stars change during their life cycle."

"We don't see much change because stars change over billions of years," adds Frank.

"My head is swelling again," moans Watson.

"All stars start out as clouds of gas and dust."

Frank and Janegoodall take turns explaining the *Life Cycle of a Star* chart.

Frank starts. "The smaller star burns its hydrogen slowly. Over time it eventually blows up to be a red giant star. Then explodes into a planetary nebula. And then it collapses into a white dwarf."

Janegoodall takes over. "A more massive star uses up its hydrogen sooner. It blows up to become a red supergiant. Then explodes in a supernova. And collapses into either a neutron star . . . or a black hole."

Watson tries to nod. "I'm pretty sure my head has now expanded into a red supergiant."

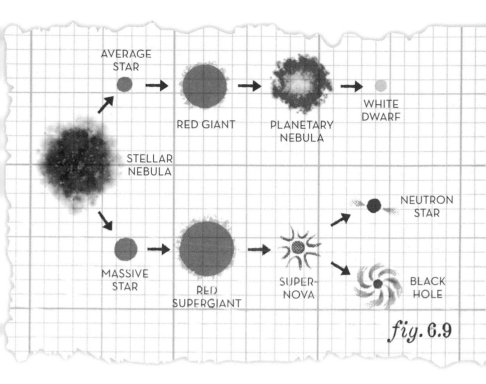

AVERAGE
STAR

RED GIANT

PLANETARY
NEBULA

WHITE
DWARF

STELLAR
NEBULA

MASSIVE
STAR

RED
SUPERGIANT

SUPER-
NOVA

NEUTRON
STAR

BLACK
HOLE

fig. 6.9

"But *this* is where it gets interesting."

Janegoodall and Frank Einstein exchange sentences like a tennis match. Watson's head swivels back and forth trying to keep up.

"It's just a theory at this time, but what if there are multiple universes?"

"With different rules?"

"With a different number of dimensions?"

"And what if they sometimes
bumped into each other?"
"Or what if they were
connected by wormholes?"

"That's it," says Watson. "My brain just exploded. The
size of the universe is just too much."

"Exactly," says Frank. "Which is why I was working on
a faster transport method. And that's how I accidentally
lost Grampa Al.

"Maybe in a wormhole . . . Maybe in a black hole . . ."

15

THE SUN RISES AT THE WESTERN END OF ELM STREET, PERFECTLY centered over the road . . . as if the street grid of Midville were some kind of modern-day Stonehenge—marking the movement of the sun and moon in the heavens, tracking the change of seasons and the passage of time. A 3-D observatory.

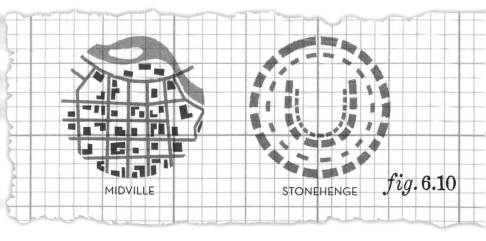

MIDVILLE   STONEHENGE   *fig.* 6.10

The rays of the sun first light up the very tops of the trees, the tallest buildings next, and then—a figure swinging in graceful arcs from telephone pole to telephone pole in the alley behind Main Street.

The acrobatic figure glides hand over hand along a wire. It hops to a tree branch. It leaps off, spins a full somersault, and lands with a *THUMP* right in front of the two robots in Grampa Al's Fix It! repair shop junkyard.

Klank jumps back in surprise.

Klink lifts his new laser-shooter arm.

"Mr. Chimp!" says Klank.

And it is.

Mr. Chimp bows.

"What are you doing here?" asks Klink. "And what do you want?"

Mr. Chimp notices the stalled hot rod model on the track. He picks it up and opens the engine compartment.

"It does not work," says Klank.

"An old gasoline engine," adds Klink. "Not worth fixing."

Mr. Chimp nods. He picks up a small wrench, adjusts a gear, resets the sparkplug.

Mr. Chimp closes the engine compartment. He sets the

car on the track, rolls the rear wheels, and starts the engine with a high-pitched whine.

Mr. Chimp releases the car. It zips around the track at top speed. Then runs out of fuel and glides to a stop.

"Wow!" says Klank.

Klink swivels his one eye. "What did you say you wanted?"

Mr. Chimp signs:

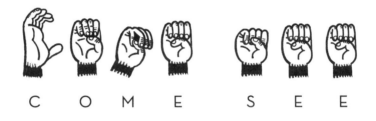

C O M E   S E E

Klank looks to Klink.
Klink nods to Klank.
They follow Mr. Chimp.

GRAMPA AL 1

THE ENTIRE WORLD STRETCHES OUT ENDLESSLY. A NEVER-ENDING collection of bits and pieces and parts and machines.

Grampa Al bends down and picks up an old wind-up alarm clock.

Hmmmm. It just needs a little fix on the gear, recoil of the spring.

Grampa Al pulls a key out of his vest pocket. He winds the clock. Sets the alarm. *Brrrrrrrriiiinnnnnnnnggggggg!* The little brass hammer wiggles back and forth, ringing the two brass bells with a high *brrrrrrrriiiinnnnnnnnggggggg!*

Grampa Al smiles, turns off the alarm.

Now, where did Frank get off to? He was here just a second ago . . .

Oh, look at that. A 1930s mechanical chimp.

Grampa Al picks it up, wondering what this little fella might need to be fixed and work again . . .

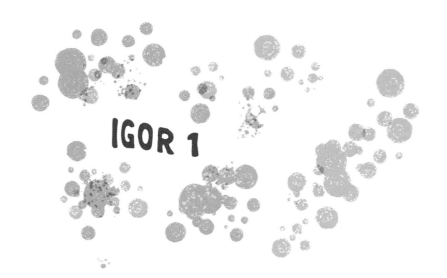

IGOR 1

THE ENTIRE WORLD STRETCHES OUT ENDLESSLY, ONE ENORMOUS soft cushion.

Warm sunlight slants down.

Igor rests his head on his front paws and purrs.

No one calls, "Come here, kitty."

No one shoos him off the table.

No one steps on his tail.

Igor stretches.

He arches his back.

He moves to a new spot, even better, even more comfortable than the last.

Igor curls into a contented ball.

And purrs. And purrs. . . .

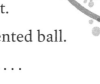

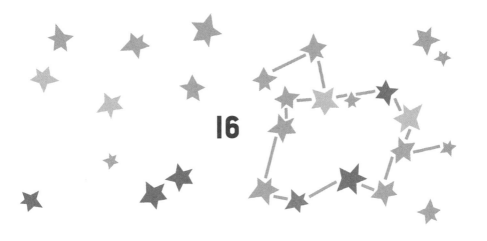

16

AVERY SMALL MAN IN COVERALLS, A WHITE HELMET LABELED
INSPECTOR, and a very large moustache strolls down
Pine Street with his hands deep in his coverall
pockets.

A stylish woman with long blond hair, walking her little
dog, approaches. She tugs on the leash, "Come on, Edith."

The moustachiocd man turns and pretends to be studying the window display of Big Joey's Plumbing & Heating
Supply.

The woman and her dog walk past, turn the corner, and
disappear.

The man resumes his slow stroll. He saunters past the
Fix It! repair shop . . . then suddenly ducks into the door-

way next door and listens. He hears a muddle of voices. He pulls a long, thin snake camera/microphone out of his pocket, attaches it to his phone, then threads the camera/mic through a gap in the old door.

The "Inspector" hides in the shadow of the doorway, listening through his earbud headphones. On his phone screen he sees three kids around a lab/worktable. One kid wearing a lab coat. A girl in a Midville Mudhens hat. The third kid digging through a backpack.

The Inspector presses **RECORD** and listens.

LabCoatKid: ". . . so what I haven't been able to figure out is how to open and close that wormhole."

MudhenKid: "Maybe there is an invention already out there that you can improve. In the same way the telescope started with simple magnifying lenses . . . that led to Galileo's first telescope . . . that led to Newton's improved reflecting telescope . . . that led to giant telescopes . . . that led to outer space telescopes like the Hubble . . . and that humongous Chinese radio telescope your mom and dad were checking out."

BackpackKid: "You really have been doing your homework."

LabCoatKid: "But space-time travel is different. No one has ever done it. Most people don't even believe it's possible."

BackpackKid: "Ha! That is the story of almost every invention. No one has ever done it. But when you make changes, additions, improvements—it's suddenly obvious."

BackpackKid pulls a stack of papers out of his backpack.

"Like check this out. 1851. A guy named Elias Howe figures out a way to 'Fasten Garments' without using buttons like everyone does.

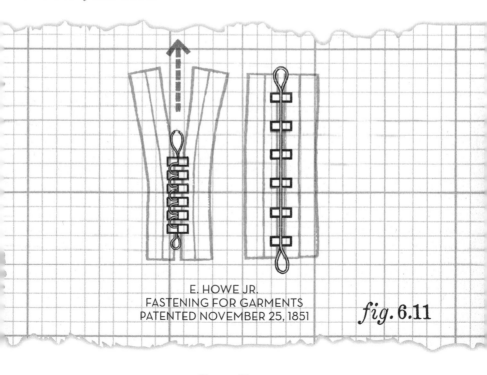

E. HOWE JR.
FASTENING FOR GARMENTS
PATENTED NOVEMBER 25, 1851

fig. 6.11

"But not much happens with it . . . until forty-two years later. 1893. Another guy—Whitcomb Judson—looking for a way faster than buttons to close shoes, improves the idea with his 'Zip Fastener.'

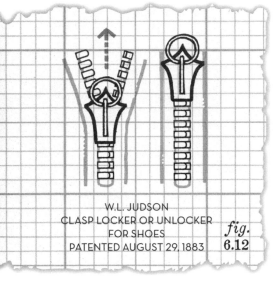

W.L. JUDSON
CLASP LOCKER OR UNLOCKER
FOR SHOES
PATENTED AUGUST 29, 1883

fig.
6.12

"The fasteners turn out to be too expensive, and they come undone too easily. So not much happens until eighteen years later, 1911, when a Swiss woman—Catharina Kuhn-Moos—makes a better slider for the fastener. And a Swedish engineer named Gideon Sundback makes better fastener teeth.

"But still, nobody wanted to buy it."

LabCoatKid: "Watson, this is the longest invention story ever. Where are you going with this?"

BackpackKid: "But Sundback kept working on the invention. In 1918, a clothing company made flying suits for the U.S. Navy using these fasteners. In 1923, the B.F. Goodrich company started using the fasteners for their rubber galoshes and decided that a good nickname for this invention, imitating the sound it made when you used it, would be . . . the zipper."

LabCoatKid and MudhenKid stare at BackpackKid.

For a moment, no one says anything.

G. SUNDBACK
SEPARABLE FASTENER
PATENTED MARCH 20, 1917 *fig.*
6.13

LabCoatKid writes something down on his papers.

LabCoatKid: "Watson and Janegoodall, you are both completely crazy . . ."

MudhenKid: "But—"

BackpackKid: "But—"

LabCoatKid: "But you are both completely brilliant. I think this just might be our genius idea."

BackpackKid: "Really?"

LabCoatKid: "Really. We just need a little improvement. A little adjustment. A new addition . . . Come on! Follow me!"

The three kids grab their jackets, run out the door to Pine Street, and don't even notice the little man in the coveralls tucking a long, thin camera device back into his pocket.

17

AHHHHHHHHHHH!" SCREAMS KLANK.

"Oooooooooooo!" beeps Klink.

Mr. Chimp stands off to one side and smiles. He pushes the long red lever forward . . . to **FULL POWER**.

Klink and Klank jump and twitch. They thrash and moan. They hop and yell. They can't take it anymore. They both blast one more giant **BEEP**, and collapse.

Mr. Chimp pulls the lever back to **PAUSE**. He stands over the two fallen robots.

Klank raises up on one elbow. He can barely speak. **"Wow."**

Klink pulls himself to sit upright, his one eye still spinning.

"I did not . . . could not . . . know . . ."

Mr. Chimp nods his head.

". . . that a robot could . . . laugh *so* hard!"

"And *feeeel* so good!" adds Klank with another laugh.

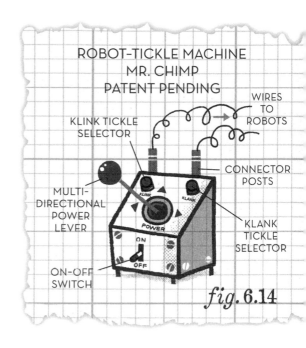

ROBOT-TICKLE MACHINE
MR. CHIMP
PATENT PENDING

WIRES TO ROBOTS

KLINK TICKLE SELECTOR

CONNECTOR POSTS

MULTI-DIRECTIONAL POWER LEVER

KLANK TICKLE SELECTOR

ON-OFF SWITCH

fig. 6.14

Mr. Chimp turns his Robot-Tickle Machine to **OFF**.

Klink sets himself upright.

Klank stands up and straightens his head.

Mr. Chimp puts an arm around Klank and gives him a pat. Klank wraps Mr. Chimp in a full body hug.

"You are my newest and very best friend!" says Klank.

"And you really understand us," adds Klink.

Mr. Chimp wiggles out of Klank's hug, and signs:

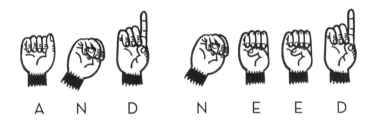

A N D N E E D

"Anything for my friend," says Klank. **"Do you want me to crush cans?"**

Mr. Chimp shakes his head.

"Klink can shoot lasers for you!"

Mr. Chimp shakes his head again. He walks over to his worktable and unrolls the plans for his Space-Time Capsule.

Klink rolls over to take a look. He scans the drawings in two seconds. "Oh, I see. You need to increase your Space-

Bend Function to smooth out your Return Warp Drive."

Mr. Chimp rechecks his drawings. He sees what Klink has instantly figured out.

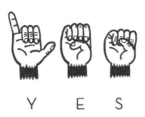

Y   E   S

Mr. Chimp leads Klink over to his Space-Time Capsule. Klink directs Klank to lift the capsule so he can start working.

"Now this is fun," beeps Klank. **"But I do have one very important question."**

Mr. Chimp turns to Klank.

"Do you have any more . . . Garfield books?"

Mr. Chimp laughs a real chimp laugh.

Mr. Chimp puts on his yellow helmet.

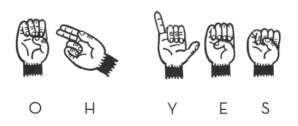

O   H   Y   E   S

FRANK EINSTEIN RUNS DOWN PINE STREET, TURNS RIGHT ON ELM Street, then left on Maple Street. Watson and Janegoodall hustle to keep up with him.

"Where are we going?" says Janegoodall.

"And what is our great idea?" asks Watson.

Frank slides to a stop in front of a shop. "Here!"

Janegoodall and Watson look up and read the shop sign.

"Sew What?"

"Yes," says Frank. "I'm sure they will have exactly what we need. The idea you have both given me to fix the Space-Time Transporter. Just what we need to get Grampa Al . . . and bring him back. Come on."

Frank swings open the old metal-and-glass door.

Janegoodall and Watson follow.

None of them notice the little man in coveralls, standing in the shadows of the building across the street, watching them.

Outside the Sew What shop, time passes.

Cars drive past. East and west.

The oversize standing street clock ticks off the seconds, one, two, three, four, five, six . . .

Overhead, white clouds drift across the blue sky.

Shadows of the buildings slowly lengthen across the street.

The man in the coveralls watches the store.

The clock ticks.

The bell to the Sew What store jangles. Frank Einstein bursts out of the store carrying a large brown-paper-wrapped package under one arm.

The small man covers his face, pretending to read a newspaper.

"Yes!" Frank calls to his friends.

Watson and Janegoodall still look a bit puzzled.

But all three of them run down the street, back toward Einstein Labs.

As soon as they round the corner, the coverall-wearing Inspector drops the newspaper and runs into Sew What.

Buttons? Fabric? Needles? The Inspector wonders what Frank Einstein could possibly need for his invention that would come from this store.

He greets the saleslady at the counter.

"Hello, I am . . . Inspector . . . Tedison. My good friends were just in here. And they need another one of whatever it is they just bought."

"Really?"

"Yes, really."

The Inspector feels his moustache sliding off one side. He quickly catches it, pressing it back on.

"Most unusual . . ."

"Yes, yes, I know. But I . . . I mean we . . . need another one. Right now."

"Hmmmmmmmmmm."

"Just in case anything happens to the first one, you know?"

The saleslady nods. "Oh, I see. That makes sense." She eyes the little man up and down once more. "Well, wait here. Let me check and see if I can find another."

She goes into the shop's back room.

The Inspector pushes his moustache back in place again.

He spots an ant walking slowly across the counter. Where is that saleslady? What is taking so long? The ant walks. She has been back there forever.

The saleslady reappears. She drops a large package on the countertop. "You are in luck! This is the last one. Folks don't usually need such a big one, you know."

"No," says the Inspector, "I'm sure they don't," having no idea what the saleslady is talking about. "But you never know when you are going to need a really big . . ."

The saleslady opens the package.

The Inspector looks, and can't help but make a weird face when he looks . . . and sees an absolutely gigantic:

"*. . . zipper?!*"

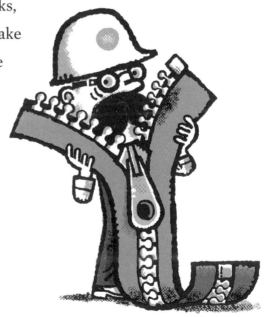

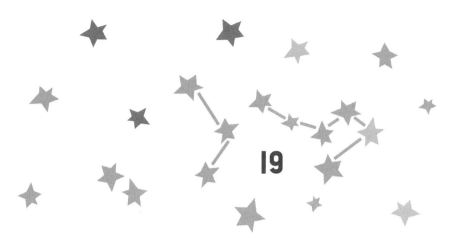

19 A

Frank Einstein clears everything off his lab workbench, and unrolls the giant zipper. "Genius! You two are complete geniuses!"

Janegoodall and Watson look around the lab. There is no one else there but them. Frank must be talking to them.

"We are?" asks Watson.

"The answer was right here in front of us." Frank digs through his shelves. "We just had to tweak the idea. Work together . . ."

Janegoodall zips and unzips the zipper. "And what exactly are we tweaking?"

"Aha!" Frank pulls out a wooden frame stretching a rubber sheet. "I'll show you." Frank sets the frame up on the table. "Einstein's theory of relativity."

"Oh, of course you will," says Watson. "And I'm guessing you don't mean your little cousin Freddy Einstein's theory."

"Very funny, Watson. But no. *The* Albert Einstein theory. From one hundred years ago. The theory that gravity is not really a force. But just a property of space-time." Frank points to the rubber sheet. "Observe—space-time."

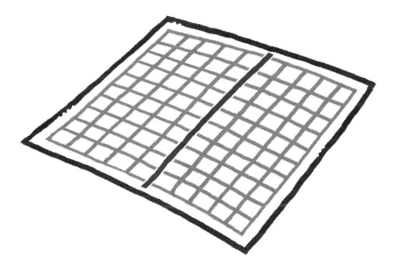

Frank rolls a small marble along a line across the sheet.

"An object in space-time moves in the straightest possible line."

Janegoodall rolls the marble straight back.

"But here's what happens around a massive object in space-time."

Frank drops a big, heavy steel ball in the middle of the sheet. It bends the rubber sheet. He rolls the same marble along the same line.

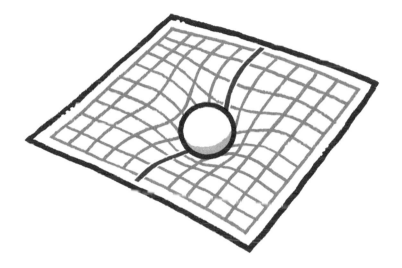

"Now the straightest possible line is curved. Gravity is not a force. It is just an effect from the way space-time is shaped. And warped."

"Whoaaaaa!" says Watson, rolling more marbles around the steel ball. "That actually makes sense."

"Now it does," says Frank. "But people didn't believe that in Einstein's time. He was the first to figure out that maybe light and space and time bend around massive objects like planets and stars."

"And that's why moons orbit around planets, and planets orbit around stars," adds Janegoodall. "Because of the shape of space-time."

"Exactly!" says Frank.

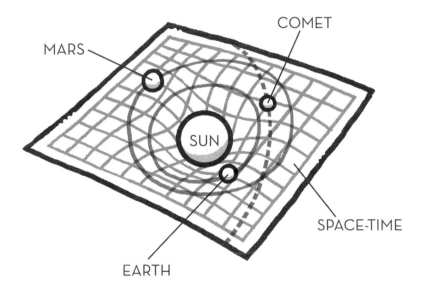

"So that's all great," says Watson, "but what the heck are we doing with this giant zipper?"

"That is your genius," says Frank. "Our tweak." He rolls the steel ball off the sheet. "We need to get from one edge of space-time to the other edge to get Grampa Al."

Frank rolls the marble across the sheet again.

"But it takes too much energy . . . and too much time to get from one side to the other."

Janegoodall rolls the marble back. "We could roll it faster."

"Can't go faster than the speed of light. Which is still too slow."

"Throw it over the sheet!" guesses Watson.

"Closer," says Frank. "What if . . ." He takes the rubber space-time sheet out of the frame and folds it over. ". . . We *folded* space-time . . ."

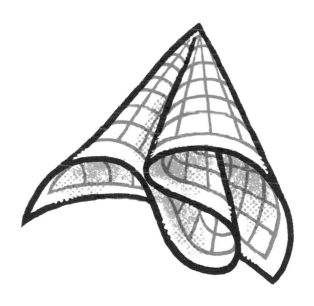

Janegoodall sees it. "Then Point A would be right next to Point B."

Frank nods. "And what if we connected the two, with something like . . ." Frank holds up the giant zipper.

Janegoodall nods. "You could go from A to B in no time!"

Watson stares at the folded sheet and the zipper.

"That is . . . completely crazy and impossible."

"Which is exactly what people said about the telescope . . . and the zipper," says Frank. "And it's why we are going to need everyone's help." Frank checks his calculations. "But we need to do this quick! Our best shot is tonight at 11:11.11."

Watson groans. "Of course it is."

Frank ignores Watson. He pulls up his Space-Time Transporter invention. "You guys start connecting these diodes to either side of the zipper. I am going to go tell Klink and Klank I am so sorry. And tell them we need them."

• • •

Unseen by any of the three, a small black wire camera and mic disappear from the crack by the door.

Outside, a small man in coveralls again tucks the snake camera inside his pocket. He hurries down the street.

Another street clock ticks . . . seeming so much faster than the other . . . toward 11:11.11.

Frank hops down the lab workshop steps two at a time to find Klink and Klank.

Frank flings opens the workshop door. "Klink and Klank, I am so sorry I forgot about you. Can you—"

Frank stops. He looks around.

He is talking to no one.

The workshop is empty.

Klink and Klank have—

vanished.

The little man in the coveralls clears everything off his lab workbench and unrolls his giant zipper.

He takes off his coveralls and his moustache.

He calls, "Mr. Chimp? Mr. Chimp! Come here! I need you."

T. Edison—because of course that's who it was this whole time—tests the zipper, then positions his titanium boxes containing the T. Edison FasterThanTheSpeedOfLight Transport Device on either side of the zipper.

He mutters to himself, "Space-time . . . curved. So why not . . . space-time folded? . . . space-time zippered? Of course! I am so glad I thought of that!"

T. Edison connects input and output wires from his boxes to either side of the zipper.

"I think I will call it—the T. Edison Space-Time Relativity Fastening and Unfastening Device."

T. Edison works, calculates, works some more. He checks the lab clock. It's getting late. He realizes he is going to need help. He calls over his shoulder, "Okay, Mr. Chimp! I am sorry I called you a brainless monkey! I will never do that again!"

From down the hall, nothing.

"Ever!"

Silence.

T. Edison zips and unzips the zipper. He checks the recording he made with his snake cam.

He reverses, forwards, and freeze-frames the video, copying Frank Einstein's plans and connections.

The clock ticks closer to 11:11.11.

"Okay," says T. Edison.

He drops the giant zipper. He picks up a shopping bag and walks down the deserted hall to Mr. Chimp's office.

"I said I'm sorry! What more do you want? A special invitation? A bag of bananas? Well, guess what I've got? Yes! A huge bag of bananas."

T. Edison swings open the door to Mr. Chimp's office.

"Now come on, we've got invention work to do."

But T. Edison is talking to no one.

Just a desk, a chair, an empty space capsule, and a stack of Garfield books.

Mr. Chimp has—

vanished.

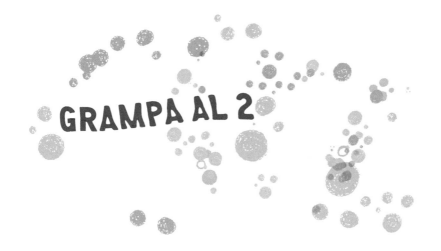

GRAMPA AL 2

THE MECHANICAL CHIMP CRASHES HIS CYMBALS *CLANG CLANG CLANG.*

Grampa Al smiles.

Fixed it!

All the little guy needed was his mainspring reset.

Grampa Al hears a whooshing noise. Its pitch goes higher and higher ... like the Doppler effect you hear when a siren is moving toward you.

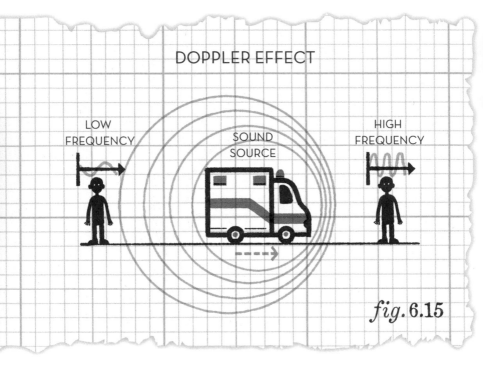

fig. 6.15

Grampa Al wonders, *What could be so loud? So large? Approaching so fast?*

What is that black dot?

IGOR 2

GOR PURRS.

Igor stretches.

Igor looks up at the lights in the sky.

The sky ahead is bluish, brighter.

The sky behind is reddish, dimmer.

Igor, being a science-smart lab-cat thinks, *That's interesting. Like the Doppler effect, which changes the pitch of sound, light changes wavelength and color when it is moving closer or farther away.*

Igor knows the increase of wavelength is called redshift.

He knows the decrease of wavelength is called blueshift.

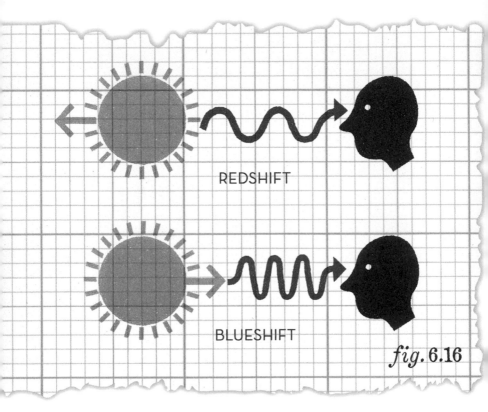

REDSHIFT

BLUESHIFT

fig. **6.16**

But Igor licks a paw and wonders,

What is moving away?

What is moving closer?

20

The clock in Frank Einstein's garage lab ticks away the seconds.

10:33.16

10:33.17

10:33.18

Frank attaches the Gravity Flow cables to both sides of the giant zipper suspended from the lab rafters.

"Where could they be?" asks Janegoodall, wiring the Light Spectrum Meter to the zipper's Lower Stop.

"No telling," answers Watson, stitching reflective silver space blankets on either side of the zipper. "Where do robots go to have fun?"

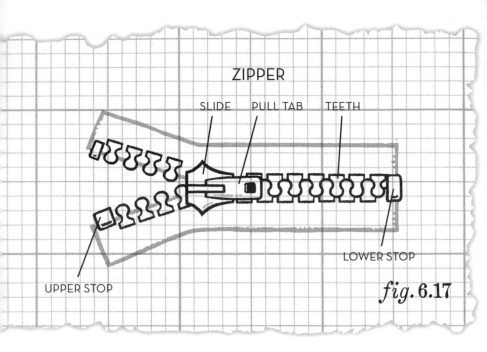

ZIPPER

SLIDE　　PULL TAB　　TEETH

LOWER STOP

UPPER STOP

fig. 6.17

"I feel like it's my fault," says Frank. "I should have told Klink we needed him."

"You shouldn't feel too bad," says Janegoodall. "Look, we made the whole zipper space transport device without their help."

"That's the other thing that worries me. I'm not sure we got the **RETURN HOME** feature right."

Klink would know. Klank would be able to test it.

The clock ticks:

11:10.33

11:10.34

11:10.35

"What?!" says Watson. "*Now* you tell us?"

"So we might find Grampa Al," says Janegoodall, "but never get back to this time and space? Or we could possibly disappear into a black hole?"

"Pretty much," says Frank. "Yeah. You don't have to go. But I'm going."

Watson and Janegoodall hesitate a beat.

"Like heck you are going alone."

"We are in."

Frank smiles.

"Okay, grab on," says Frank Einstein. "Ready or not—here is the Space-Time Zipper!"

"I don't really love that 'or not' part," says Watson nervously.

All three grab the Space-Time Zipper Pull Tab.

The clock ticks:

11:11.09

11:11.10

11:11.11

The lab lights dim blue. The zipper lights pure white.

"*Now!*"

Frank, Janegoodall, and Watson yank down the Space-Time Zipper Pull Tab.

And disappear.

The clock in the ChimpEdison Laboratories ticks away the seconds.

10:33.16

10:33.17

10:33.18

T. Edison attaches the Gravity Flow cables to both sides of the giant zipper suspended from the frame.

"Where could that stupid monkey be?" T. Edison mutters, wiring the Light Spectrum Meter to the zipper's Bottom Box Stop.

T. Edison stitches reflective silver space blankets on either side of the zipper. "Where do monkeys go to have fun?"

T. Edison loops the last stitch.

"It's not my fault he's missing out on such a great invention."

He clears the table.

"Though I don't feel too bad."

T. Edison stands back and admires his handiwork.

"Look, I've made this whole T. Edison Space-Time Relativity Fastening and Unfastening Device without his help."

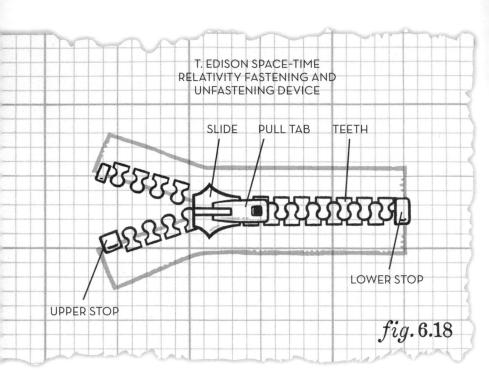

T. EDISON SPACE-TIME
RELATIVITY FASTENING AND
UNFASTENING DEVICE

SLIDE   PULL TAB   TEETH

LOWER STOP

UPPER STOP

fig. **6.18**

T. Edison tosses Mr. Chimp's book in the corner.

"I'm brilliant. I'm sure I've got every bit of this right!"

The clock ticks:

11:10.33

11:10.34

11:10.35

"I will find that idiot cat, too. And make millions off this invention. And everyone will know my name. Pretty much forever."

T. Edison smiles at the thought.

"Okay. Ready for my . . . T. Edison Space-Time Relativity Fastening and Unfastening Device."

T. Edison grabs the T. Edison Space-Time Relativity Fastening and Unfastening Device Pull Tab.

The clock ticks:

11:11.09

11:11.10

11:11.11

The lab lights dim blue.

The T. Edison Space-Time Relativity Fastening and Unfastening Device lights up pure electromagnetic white.

"*Now!*"

T. Edison yanks down the T. Edison Space-Time Relativity Fastening and Unfastening Device Pull Tab.

And disappears.

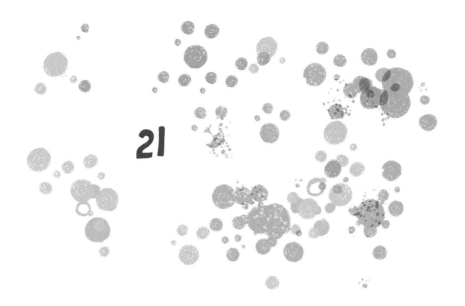

THE FIRST THING FRANK NOTICES IS THE SUN MOVING, TWISTING, changing shapes.

The second thing Frank notices is Watson and Janegoodall moving, twisting, changing shapes.

"Whoaaaaaa!" says Watson. "Frank! Your head is all blobby!"

Janegoodall laughs. "Look who's talking, crazy-feet Watson!"

Frank waves a multiple hand through the air. "Check this out—we can see blood moving inside us, electrical nerve paths, cells growing and collapsing . . ."

Watson picks up a leafy tree branch. "Why am I seeing this as a seed and a tree and as dead wood?"

"Time is just another dimension," says Frank. "Like height and width and depth. We are in the right place."

Janegoodall's head stretches to a long, thin oval . . . and then disappears. "And what place is that? With Einstein in Wonderland?"

"Kind of," says Frank. "We are in a parallel universe. With an entry somewhere near Alpha Andromedae. We are seeing in four and five and maybe six dimensions. This is where I lost Grampa Al."

Watson spirals off into a fractal shape.

"Well, we better find him quick! 'Cause I am about to lose my lunch . . . in all four or five or six dimensions."

CLANG CLANG CLANG.

A shape-shifting me-chanical monkey bangs his cymbals in waves of purple, then breaks.

"Meooooowww," calls a cat.

"Follow those!" calls an amoeba-looking Frank.

Flexible morphing through space and time and multiple dimensions, Janegoodall and Watson follow Frank down through around back over into below past a rainbow-light-shifting spot.

"*Helllllp!*" yells what looks like a hairy mushroom on top of a pair of tiny wingtip shoes.

"T. Edison?" guesses half-transparent Janegoodall.

"Ooook ooook!" calls a starburst of chimpanzee arms and legs up in a waving tree.

"Mr. Chimp!" says still-fractal Watson.

A large robot with a colander head steps from behind the tree. **"Lasagna!"**

The smaller robot behind him rolls his webcam eye. "Oh boy."

"Klink and Klank!" calls melting-Frank. He gives them both a hug. "What are you guys doing here?"

"Space-time traveling, same as you," says Klink.

"Could this get any weirder?" asks Watson.

A Janegoodall laugh echo-warps and boomerangs around. She looks over what would usually be Watson's shoulder.

"Oh yes, things could get weirder. Hello, Einstein."

A geometric manshape stroking a floating tabby cat head floats down next to the four kids, two robots, and one chimpanzee.

"Hello, Einstein."

"Grampa Al!" yells Frank, oozing over into his grandpa's folding arms.

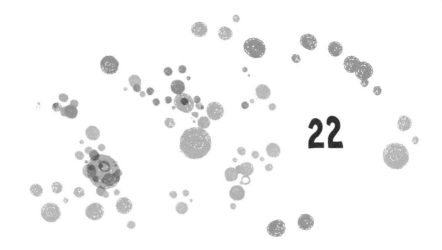

22

FRANK EINSTEIN, GRAMPA AL, WATSON, AND JANEGOODALL WOBBLE and expand and contract and attach to one another in a shimmering cluster of soap bubbles group hug.

"I can't believe we found you," blips Watson's bubble mouth.

"Frank has only been gone for ten minutes," pops dome-head Grampa Al.

"Which has been twenty-four hours back on Earth," wiggles Janegoodall.

"Ahhhh, space-time dilation," beams Grampa Al.

"Meooow," confirms floating cat-head Igor.

Expanded Frank turns a swirl of colors. "And we used that twenty-four hours to improve the Space-Time Transporter . . . and change it into a Space-Time Zipper."

"Great!" says half of Grampa Al's spiraling head, eyeballing a suspicious kaleidoscope of jagged shapes in the distance. "Because something big is headed this way. And I think we should get out of this 4-D universe before it gets here."

"This is a 7-D universe," reports Klink. "You are seeing seven dimensions."

Klank pouts. "No fun for us. Because we are only built to see three dimensions."

Watson shakes his pulsing head in disbelief. "I have no idea what any of that means. But I'm with Grampa Al—let's get busy and get out of here."

"Right," says Frank. "We just need to reset the Space-Time Zipper." Frank holds up the Pull Tab of the Space-Time Zipper. "Ohhhh no."

The Space-Time Zipper Pull Tab is not attached to anything.

"Heeeeeelp!" squeals the spinning blob on the wing-tip shoes.

"T. Edison!" calls Frank. "We know you copied our invention. But for once, you can do something good. We can use your Space-Time Zipper."

"It is a T. Edison Space-Time Relativity Fastening and Unfastening Device," T. EdisonFungus answers. "And I thought of it all by myself."

"Yeah, sure you did," says Watson. "We don't care what you call it. Let's set it up!"

T. Edison holds up his invention's Zipper Teeth. But T. Edison's Zipper Teeth are likewise . . . attached to nothing.

"Noooooo," says Janegoodall.

"Klink and Klank! How did you and Mr. Chimp get here?"

Mr. Chimp somersaults down from the overhead branch in what looks like a series of time-lapse photography.

Klink answers, "We modified the NASA space capsule used by Mr. Chimp's grandfather."

"And I helped, too!" says Klank.

"Fantastic!" says Frank. "Maybe we can use that. In sequence."

The sky darkens and the kaleidoscope spins.

Mr. Chimp holds up his lever control box. Attached to nothing.

Watson pops. "Oh man! Three space-time travel inventions? And all three of them are busted. Could this get any worse?"

"Meoooow," warns Igor's waving head, looking toward the approaching dark shape.

"Yes, it could," says Janegoodall. "Because that approaching funnel of darkness looks exactly like what we did *not* want to run into—a black hole."

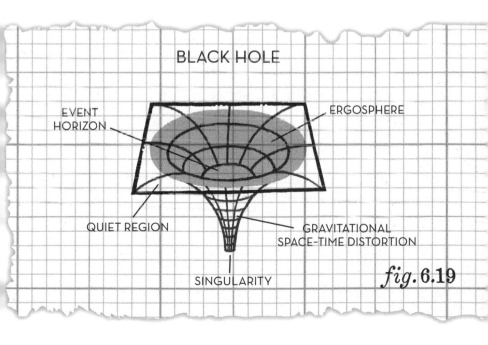

BLACK HOLE

EVENT HORIZON

ERGOSPHERE

QUIET REGION

GRAVITATIONAL SPACE-TIME DISTORTION

SINGULARITY

fig. **6.19**

23

C *RRRRRRRRRRRRRAAAAAAAAAAAAAAASSSSSSSSSSSSSSSHHHHHHHHHHHH*
Wwwwwwwhhhhhhhhoooooooossssssshhhhhhh
Sssssspiiiiinnnnn, mmmmmeeeeellllltttt,
ooooozzzzze . . .

The bubble cluster of friends and enemies and robots huddles in the middle of the worsening seven-dimensional cyclone.

Colors shapes sounds/height width depth/past present future, all twist and flash and spin around them.

"Klink! Klank!" yells Watson, unraveling. "What do we do?"

"Hmmmm." Klink quickly calculates all possibilities. "I do not have any answers for this problem."

Klank shakes in 3-D fright. **"Lasagna? A nap?"** Frank Einstein thinks.

"I'll be danged," says Grampa Al. "Never seen anything like this. No way to escape. This might be the end."

The approaching black hole warps space and light and time.

"It's not like a black hole sucks you into anything," Jane-goodall explains. "It's more like all space-time goes over a waterfall.

"And once we go over that waterfall, we can't swim out faster than the speed of light that we are falling in."

"Oh, that makes me feel sooo much better," says Watson. "Aieeeeeeeeee! Now I am really freaking out!"

Watson splits into a twirl of Watsons.

FunhouseMirror Frank Einstein thinks.

"Maybe . . ."

"Maybe what?"

"Just like you said before, build on what everyone has done . . . use everyone . . . Klink and Klank, Janegoodall, Watson, T. Edison, and Mr. Chimp. *And* . . . the energy of the black hole itself."

• • •

Crrrrrrrrrrrraaaaaaaaaaaassssssssssssssssshhhhhhh . . .
Wwwwwwwhhhhhhhhoooooooossssssshhhhhhh . . .
"If we all work together, I think we have one shot at this.
"Or we waterfall into nothing."
Frank sketches out his plan in the inky air, using his headhand.
Everyone else is all eyes.
And ears.
Really.

24

"**O**K, WE USE T. EDISON'S TEETH, PULL TAB, AND LOWER STOP."

"I doubt this invention will work," says T. Edison, handing over his zipper teeth.

"Janegoodall, can you rethread our Pull Tab?"

"Yes."

"Watson—you and Grampa Al rewire both Power Cables into the Upper Stop."

"On it."

"Klank—can you hold the whole thing up across those branches?"

"Does Garfield like to sleep in?" Klank picks up the giant Zipper. **"I just hope I don't get blown up like I always do."**

The space-time cyclone howls louder.

The light begins to shift.

Janegoodall looks up. "Aaaaand that is not a good sign."

"Klink," says Frank.

"Yes, that is my name," says a still slightly miffed Klink.

"We need you most of all."

That brightens up Klink.

"To make this space-time fold, we are going to need massive power."

"Obviously."

"We use Einstein's most famous formula." Frank points to the black hole looming. "And tap into the most massive object in the universe."

Klink lights up at the thought. "Oh yes. Then the energy will be equal to the incredible mass of the black hole, times the very fast speed of light squared."

$$E = mc^2$$

"Exactly!" beams lightbulb Frank. "But how do we connect?"

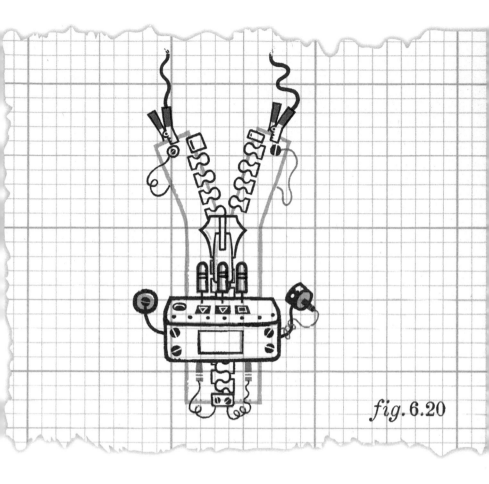

fig. 6.20

Klink whirrs and blinks. And whirrs once more.

The sky turns a deep purple.

A whirling tornado of Klink ideas twist overhead, then spin down a drain.

"Ooook," says a now-glowing Mr. Chimp.

Klink nods his glass-dome head. "`Ooook` is exactly right."

Frank turns into a question mark.

Mr. Chimp holds up his grampa Ham's old space capsule control board.

Frank turns into an exclamation point. "Of course!"

Klink continues, "But if you connect—"

"Oooooh ooooh ook," Mr. Chimp stops Klink.

Klink understands. Klink nods.

"Can you do it?" asks Frank Einstein.

Mr. Chimp signs:

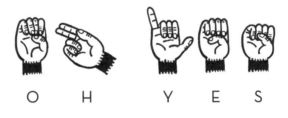

O   H   Y   E   S

• • •

Stars above begin to wink out, waterfalling into the black hole.

"Any time now would be good," says Janegoodall.

Mr. Chimp leaps into action. He wires the antique control panel into place. He somersaults up to the top of the

waving tree with cables of pure blue light. He waves OK.

"This is either genius . . . or pure crazy," says Grampa Al.

Watson's eyes bug out. "Thanks for that cheerful thought."

Space-time creaks, crackles, builds to a roaring crescendo.

"Ready, everyone?" Frank yells over the din. "Klank, grab the Pull Tab. Yank it on my count to zero!"

Frank takes one last look at the 7-D universe. His closest friends. His fiercest enemies. His robot pals. Their past, present, future weaving a tapestry of space-time.

He hears Albert Einstein:

"Death signifies nothing . . . the distinction between past, present, and future is only a stubbornly persistent illusion."

Frank Einstein nods, then counts, "Five, four, three, two, one . . . *pull!*"

Klank pulls.

Mr. Chimp leaps into the heavens on bolts of blue.

Everything goes white.

Then black.

25

THE SUN SETS SLOWLY IN THE WESTERN SKY OF MIDVILLE.

In the junkyard behind Grampa Al Einstein's Fix It! repair shop and Frank Einstein's laboratory, just above the storm sewer behind the washing machine and junker car, nothing moves.

The last red-orange rays of the star that Earth orbits light the top of the giant maple tree in the alley.

Venus, Jupiter, and a crescent moon track their paths, as ever, across the evening sky.

In motion too slow for the human eye to track, the stars of constellations spin overhead.

The solar system twirls.

The Milky Way galaxy spins.

Stars are born, grow, collapse, die.

Back in the junkyard, still nothing.

Sometimes plans don't work out.

Oftentimes inventions fail.

Who can know how things work out?

There is a theory that every possibility works out.

That there are multiple universes.

An infinite number of universes.

One for every combination of possibilities.

For the universe where you didn't make the bus this morning, you missed the class on stars, you weren't inspired to become a scientist, and the world didn't get the

invention that you would go on to make, which would change everything . . .

But in this universe, in this moment, in the junkyard behind Grampa Al's Fix It! repair shop and Frank Einstein's laboratory—

Nothing.

No one.

26

UNTIL *ZZZZZZZZZZZZZZZZZIIIIIIIIIIIIIIIIIIIIIPPPPPPPPPPPPPPPP!*

At precisely 08:08.08, the yellow lightbulbs of the junkyard arrow sign suddenly flash, then light up in sequence. Blinking. Pointing.

The space-time just above the picnic table unzips . . . and a jumble of bodies and robots and starlight and cosmic dust crashes out into this world.

Watson conks his head against the busted washing machine with a bonk and an "Owwwwww!"

"Whooo hoooo! We did it!" cheers Janegoodall, sitting on top of the junker car.

T. Edison crawls out from under a pile of old bicycles. "I told you it would only work . . . if you used my part of the invention."

Grampa Al, sitting on top of the pile of vacuums, legs crossed, laughs and laughs, and laughs some more.

Klink rolls out from under a pile of old cans. "Exactly as I had calculated."

Frank Einstein, standing on top of the MIDVILLE STORM SEWER cover, beams. "Exactly." He looks around the junkyard, never happier to be in the middle of all of this junk. In the middle of his friends. In the beginning of his life. "And we did it with help from everyone."

Frank holds a piece of pipe like a scepter.

"Thank you, Watson. Thank you, Janegoodall. Thank you, Grampa Al. Thank you, T. Edison. Thank you, Klink. Thank you . . . Klank?"

Frank and everyone look around the junkyard.

"Klank."

No Klank.

"Klank!"

A noise, a bent piece of aluminum siding moves.

"Mmmrmrmnkjfkhfk."

"What is that?!"

"The 7-D jumble has fallen into our universe!"

"Smash it!"

Frank edges his pipe under the siding.

"Mjsdvijisjijhsfihiuh."

Frank takes a deep breath, flips the siding over, and raises his pipe to bash the 7-D invader back to its own world.

"Hoooorah! We did it!" cheers a colander robot head.

"Klank!" Frank yells in relief.

"We did it, we did it, we did it. And I did not get blown up."

Frank bends down.

"I cannot believe it. I am perfectly OK."

Frank smiles. "Yes, you are, Klank. A couple quick fixes . . . and you'll be good as new."

Frank picks up Klank's body-less head and puts it on the picnic table.

"Fantastic," says Klank's head. **"And—lasagna!"**

Grampa Al and Watson and Janegoodall laugh.

"But where is Mr. Chimp?"

"Mr. Chimp!" calls T. Edison.

Klink points up to the heavens. More specifically to the Andromeda galaxy in the northern sky.

"Mr. Chimp knew he was not coming back. He is in his own universe now."

Igor the cat meows.

"I always knew that monkey was his own . . . monkey," says T. Edison proudly.

"Ape," Janegoodall corrects T. Edison.

Frank helps Grampa Al down from the pile of vacuums.

"Thanks, Einstein."

"No. Thank you, Einstein. Thanks for helping us think like scientists. Because now, more than ever, we are going to need to be scientists."

"Oh no," says Watson. "Why?"

Frank Einstein looks up at the stars, planets, galaxies spinning above them. He hears Albert Einstein again:

"Once an event occurs, it becomes
part of the fabric of the Universe.
We make our own mark on the Universe.
Our actions create space-time Universes.
We need to take care of our Universes."

"Because now Mr. Chimp has shown us that we can explore and discover and take care of . . . a whole universe of universes."

MATTER

ENERGY

HUMANS

Aristotle

newton

daVinci

$E = mc^2$

Tesla

FRANK EINSTEIN'S COSMIC ADDRESS

Frank Einstein Workshop and Laboratory
The Junkyard behind Grampa Al's Fix It! Repair Shop
And the Old Garage next to it
11235 Pine Street

• Filled with twenty years' worth of mechanical, electrical, and plumbing parts, appliances, and tools.

• Also piano keyboards, watches, toasters, webcams, hamburger grills, stomach exercisers, TV remotes, magnets, aluminum flex-duct hoses, batteries, locks, speakers, Shop-Vac, wheels, a glass dome, a silver trash can, an old stove, tongs, a colander, wires, screws, bolts, nails, lights, vacuum cleaners, bicycles, radios, a few cars, springs, chains, locks, and a broken HugMeMonkey! doll.

• Frank Einstein's Workshop and Laboratory is part of the larger Town of Midville.

THE TOWN OF MIDVILLE

- In the middle of the United States of America.
- Population 6,543.
- 7.3 miles across.
- Home of Frank Einstein pals Watson and Janegoodall.
- Also home of T. Edison, Mr. Chimp, and the T. Edison Laboratories (later renamed ChimpEdison Laboratories).
- Also home of the Midville Mud Hens baseball stadium, Midville City Hall, Lake Midville, the Midville Dam, the Midville Forest Preserve, the Midville Power and Light Company, and Midville Park.
- The Town of Midville is part of the larger Planet Earth.

PLANET EARTH

- Formed over 4 billion years ago.
- 7,928 miles around its middle.
- The only planet with liquid water on its surface and an atmosphere containing 21% oxygen.
- Not an exact sphere—more a slightly squashed sphere.
- 93 million miles from the sun, it orbits in 365 ¼ days.
- Spins around on its axis once every 24 hours, making daytime on its side facing the sun, nighttime on its side facing away.
- The Planet Earth is part of the larger Solar System.

THE SOLAR SYSTEM

- Composed of
  - The Sun, a giant gas-burning star
  - 8 planets: Mercury, Venus, Earth, Mars, Jupiter, Saturn, Uranus, and Neptune
  - And lots of dwarf planets, moons, asteroids, meteroids, and comets.
- 1 million Earths could fit inside the Sun.
- The Solar System is over 7 billion (7,000,000,000) miles across.
- Ancient man used to believe that everything revolved around the Earth. Scientists discovered that everything actually revolves around the Sun.
- 4 inner "terrestrial" planets (Mercury, Venus, Earth, Mars) are made up of mostly rock and metal.
- 2 outer "gas giants" (Jupiter and Saturn) are made up of mostly hydrogen and helium gas.
- 2 outer "ice giants" (Uranus and Neptune) are made up of mostly ice forms of water, ammonia, and methane.
- The Solar System is part of the larger Milky Way Galaxy.

THE MILKY WAY GALAXY

- The Milky Way Galaxy is not the biggest, or the smallest galaxy. But it is an impressive 120,000 light-years across. And it contains over 200 billion stars.

- Our Solar System is located about 27,000 light-years from the center of the Galaxy, on the inner edge of one of the 4 spiral arms.

- It's called the Milky Way because the collection of stars we see from Earth looks like a milky smear in the night sky.

- Like most large galaxies, the Milky Way has a supermassive black hole (SMBH) at its center. This SMBH is *4.6 million* times the mass of our Sun!

- The Milky Way Galaxy is part of the larger Laniakea Supercluster.

YOU ARE HERE

THE LANIAKEA SUPERCLUSTER

- In 2014, a group of astronomers at the University of Hawaii figured out a way to map galaxies by looking at their motion.
- This makes our Milky Way Galaxy part of this supercluster of over 100,000 galaxies.
- Our Laniakea Supercluster stretches out over 520 million light years.
- The galaxies of Supercluster are pulled toward the dense center called the Great Attractor.
- "Laniakea" means "Immeasurable Heaven" in Hawaiian. This name was chosen to honor Polynesian navigators who used their knowledge of the heavens to navigate the Pacific Ocean.
- The Laniakea Supercluster is part of the larger Observable Universe.

YOU ARE
HERE

THE OBSERVABLE UNIVERSE

- The Universe is all of space-time and all of its contents. Superclusters, galaxies, solar systems, planets, towns, homes, people. Everything.
- The Observable Universe is estimated to be 90.68 billion light-years across.
- Gravity is the biggest force in the large scale of the Universe.
- The Universe is a web of Superclusters. Some parts of the Universe are densely packed. Others are almost empty.
- The Universe is expanding, at an ever-increasing rate. We don't really know why.

LOCAL
SUPERCLUSTERS

YOU ARE HERE

THE MULTIVERSE

- There is a theory that our Universe is just one of a set of disconnected universes.
- Each other universe could have different physical laws, and even different numbers of dimensions from ours.
- You can think of the Multiverse as a bunch of space-times, not interconnected, but still existing. Like a group of soap bubbles. Observers in any one soap bubble would be unable to interact with observers in any of the other soap bubbles.
- The size, and idea, of the Multiverse is just mind-blowing.

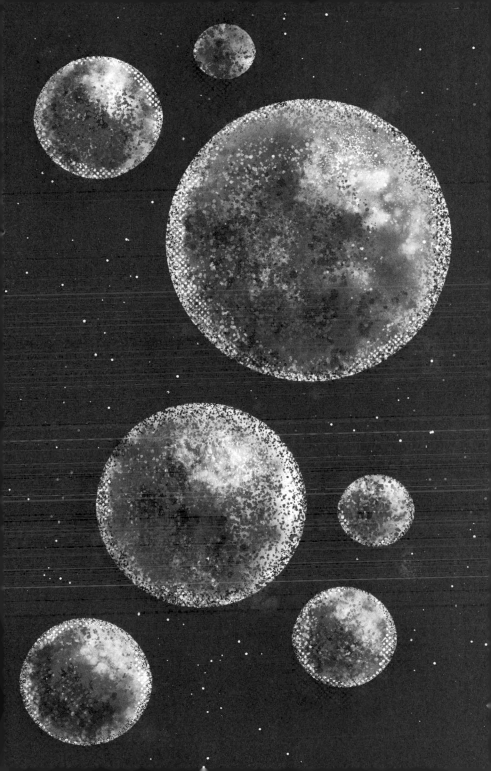

Frank Einstein

11235 Pine Street

Town of Midville

United States of America

Earth

Sol System

Milky Way Galaxy

Laniakea Supercluster

The Universe

?????????

MR. CHIMP'S ALPHABET

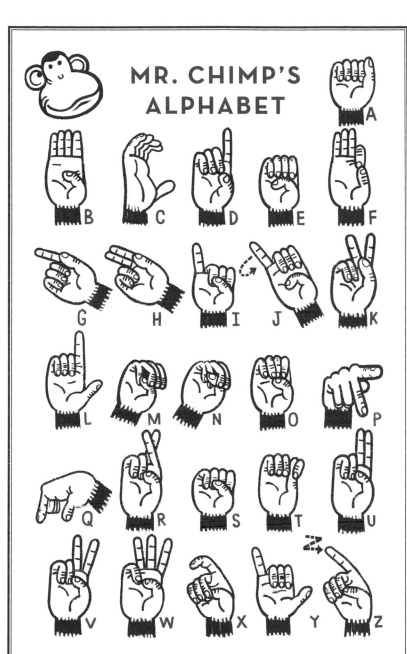

Antimatter Motor

Electro-Finger

BrainTurbo

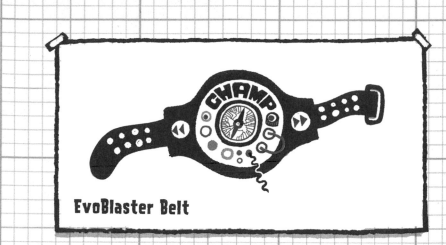

EvoBlaster Belt

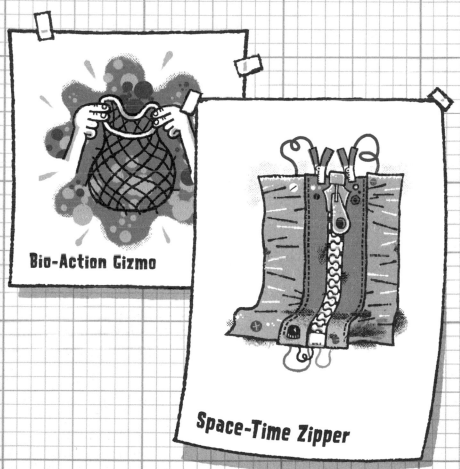

Bio-Action Gizmo

Space-Time Zipper

JON SCIESZKA lives in many universes. In writing this book, he lived in an alternate Universe not connected with the Universe and space-time which contains this book. You will have to ask him how he managed that.

BRIAN BIGGS has illustrated an infinite number of books over an infinite number of years, including the Tinyville Town series. He works in a studio in Philadelphia, Pennsylvania, that is basically a black hole of art supplies and obsolete computer parts, and he regularly goes back in time to his sixth-grade-self to remind him to eat his vegetables and get a little exercise. Brian would like to thank Jon Scieszka and the Abrams team for the opportunity to draw robots for the last four years.

TO THE INQUISITIVE AND FEARLESS
MR. CHIMP AND ALBERT EINSTEIN
IN ALL OF US.

LIBRARY OF CONGRESS CATALOGING-IN-PUBLICATION DATA
NAMES: SCIESZKA, JON, AUTHOR. | BIGGS, BRIAN, ILLUSTRATOR.
TITLE: FRANK EINSTEIN AND THE SPACE-TIME ZIPPER / BY JON SCIESZKA;
ILLUSTRATED BY BRIAN BIGGS.
DESCRIPTION: NEW YORK : AMULET BOOKS, 2018. | SERIES: FRANK EINSTEIN ; BOOK 6 |
SUMMARY: "FRANK EINSTEIN (KID-GENIUS, SCIENTIST, AND INVENTOR) AND HIS BEST FRIEND,
WATSON, ALONG WITH KLINK (A SELF-ASSEMBLED ARTIFICIAL-INTELLIGENCE ENTITY) AND
KLANK (A *MOSTLY* SELF-ASSEMBLED AND ARTIFICIAL *ALMOST* INTELLIGENCE ENTITY), ONCE
AGAIN FIND THEMSELVES IN COMPETITION WITH T. EDISON, THEIR CLASSMATE AND ARCHRIVAL,
THIS TIME STUDYING THE SCIENCE AND MYSTERIES OF THE UNIVERSE!"
—PROVIDED BY PUBLISHER.
IDENTIFIERS: LCCN 2017052440 | ISBN 978-1-4197-2547-0 (HARDCOVER)
SUBJECTS: | CYAC: INVENTORS—FICTION. | ROBOTS—FICTION. | SPACE AND TIME—
FICTION. | HUMOROUS STORIES. | SCIENCE FICTION. | BISAC: JUVENILE FICTION / SCIENCE &
TECHNOLOGY. | JUVENILE FICTION / ROBOTS. | JUVENILE FICTION / HUMOROUS STORIES.
CLASSIFICATION: LCC PZ7.S41267 FV 2018 | DDC [FIC]—DC23

PRINTED AND BOUND IN U.S.A.
10 9 8 7 6 5 4 3 2 1

ABRAMS The Art of Books
195 Broadway, New York, NY 10007
abramsbooks.com

ALSO AVAILABLE IN PAPERBACK

"PROVES THAT SCIENCE CAN BE AS FUN AS IT IS IMPORTANT AND USEFUL." —*PUBLISHERS WEEKLY*